1

Gun-whipped!

The shores of the lake were dark and shadowed. Timber grew almost to the water's edge. It was also late, just minutes short of midnight, but the old man had ridden and tramped the country roundabout in years past and knew the winding trail to Vickers' cabin.

An owl hooted; somewhere a long way off, a pair of mountain cats wailed; nearby a stream gurgled, running over a steep and rocky bed to the lake. Else it was silent and the man could easily believe he was the only human soul within miles.

He'd left his horse tied to a tree a half-mile back. His advance was surreptitious, announced to no one by the soft crunch of waxed calf, military-style, full wellington boots on the fallen pine needles, or the slight heaviness that exertion in advancing years — nigh on sixty — brought to his breathing.

He drew in deep lungfuls of the damp earth smell and the heady tree scent.

He studied on his behavior. If there'd been folks to see it, they would have considered it odd, for sure. Why should a lonely old man be spying on Sheriff Vickers?

Maybe they'd just think it was him — senile Robert McGill: 'Crazy Bob.' He knew how the citizens of Redstone on whose outskirts he now lived were apt, when they thought he wasn't looking, to tap their foreheads solemnly. Not mad but not normal, they'd mouth to one another . . . or words to that effect.

Then again, they might put it down to voyeurism. Daniel Vickers was also called a name behind his back: 'Dirty Dan.'

According to the official story put

about the town, the lakeside cabin was the sheriff's occasional fishing retreat, where he went on a weekend when he had a hankering to relax away from the cares of office. But it was also known that Vickers was a ladies' man, a Fancy Dan with a taste for the finest: well-tailored clothing, high-stakes poker games, good whiskey and — a badly kept town secret — the likes of young and fresh saloon girls.

Invariably, a comely female was also absent a spell from Redstone coinciding with Vickers' sojourns up at the lake, and it was never his wife, Sophie. She professed no love of fishing.

Sophie's love was her haberdashery shop behind which she and Vickers, childless, had lived in comfortable rooms some eight years. In her late thirties, she did share Vickers' taste for fine clothes. She had a very full closet of them and a figure to show them off. Vickers no longer seemed to notice. Maybe he never had. Their marriage had been political; of convenience to

Sophie's father and Vickers' larger ambitions.

Bob McGill reckoned it a damned shame Dan Vickers couldn't stick to what was morally and legally his and required constant novelty. And the shame had turned especially and personally grave for McGill. He was filled with heavy, nameless dread.

He suspected he might know the young woman with whom Vickers was sharing his latest adulterous escapade. But suspicion was not enough for him to speak up. Though he thought it might break his old heart, finding out for sure who she might be was the purpose of his furtive night mission. He'd ridden some hard saddles in his lifetime, but none harder than this.

Beyond the timber to the north a bleak mountain thrust its snow-capped peak into the night sky, luminous in the moonlight, but it was plenty dark where the trees grew together overhead. McGill flitted as best as rheumatic limbs allowed from one patch of deep shadow to another till the lap of the water on the lake's shingle beach grew audible.

Lamplight made a yellow square in the dark, log-walled bulk of Vickers' cabin, which was a silhouette against the silver shimmers of the lake.

McGill set course for the window, darting across the last open space with all possible speed to come up close to the wall. The window was partly open. He heard voices inside — one man's, one woman's — and he raised up to look inside.

* * *

'Go on, woman, do it. It won't kill you.'

Dan Vickers chuckled at the expression of distaste that crossed his companion's face. 'And remember, it's for the sake of your dear husband. It has his specific sanction. Whatever I ask, he told you!'

At this point he laughed out loud.

Liberty, who was on her knees before

5

him, said nothing. She employed her mouth otherwise, as he'd indicated. Far better that she should co-operate than be forcibly choked. The sheriff would do as he pleased anyway. Besides, she'd grown accustomed to doing as she was ordered, whether she liked it or not.

She always toed the mark when Tom told her to do something. This occasion, she might have said to Tom justifiably, 'No, not this time. You've pushed me too far. I won't go with this man, even if it is to save your neck.'

But she hadn't.

What good would it have availed her if she had?

Liberty knew she'd been on a slide to hell just weeks after she'd married Tom Tolliver, but she'd decided it took a woman considerable less pride than she possessed to renounce her vows and quit. More courage, too.

On a practical level she was aware, as all wives were, that society and its leaders condemned women who repudiated the concept of a man's ultimate authority over his spouse and household.

After the bloodbath of the War Between the States and the emancipation of the slaves, many influential Americans chose as their goal nationwide spiritual and moral revival. They were motivated by growing concerns over obscenity, abortion, sex without the sanction of marriage, the changing role of women in society, and the increased procreation by the lower classes these sins occasioned.

Meanwhile, the Catholic Church condemned as evils birth control and abortion. States began enacting laws that made it more difficult to divorce and gave single people greater incentive to marry.

In New York City in 1872, twenty-nine-year-old Anthony Comstock became head of a Society for the Suppression of Vice. His campaign was financed by some of the wealthiest and most influential philanthropists. These men had a broad definition of vice. Comstock used their money to lobby the State Legislature for laws which, while criminalizing sex outside of marriage, also included much else, such as restrictions on what could be sent through the mails. Twenty-four states passed similar prohibitions which were known collectively as the Comstock laws.

In this climate, women of the West like Liberty were denied information on even the basics, like family planning. Commonly, their hard lives turned them into drudges. Though outnumbered by men, and therefore prized by them, they were also vulnerable to exploitation. Their comforts came courtesy of the men, who upheld the letter of the law yet often perverted the moral code that informed it.

Beyond the rigors of housekeeping and home-making, the expectation was that women should do their duty, ask no questions, and above all obey. They were cut off from communication with their sisters, from enlightenment and education, living in harsh, often lonely rural conditions.

To Liberty, marriage had once seemed a good idea. She'd had no one else to rely on, other than an aging father of odd habits and declining fortunes.

Tom Tolliver, although many years her senior — in his middle years, in fact — had a small ranch and therefore a living. He also had an air of bonhomie she now realized should have appealed only in a younger man yet to achieve maturity. Tolliver's apparent flair was no more than garrulousness and shiftlessness. It was cheerful foolery in company that won him the ladies' favor.

It was Liberty's own silly mistake that she'd allowed him to charm his way into a marriage he'd subsequently proved he didn't deserve.

He shied away from hard work and decisions. Caught in any fix, he lacked backbone. His property was mean — a log shack, a pole-and-brush shed and a brush corral. Nothing to be proud of.

And though he'd been savage in

carrying out her sexual initiation, Tom Tolliver later proved nigh on impotent as well as a general loser.

But by then the damage was done. She'd always had a good measure of self-confidence as a child, but her wedding-night 'breaking in', as Tolliver termed it, had stolen much of it.

A pretty young girl should have made a wiser match, but she'd done her best to make a home and bring comfort to the crude log shack. She'd tried to save herself from becoming a slattern.

That she'd succeeded had contributed to her present predicament.

While Liberty had been hard at work, without which the marriage would have long since failed, her husband had been caught redhanded by Sheriff Vickers crudely altering a brand on a Flying L yearling to a Rocking T with a running iron.

The Lant family, who owned the Flying L, ruled the roost in the Redstone Gulch country. Worse, Vickers was their man.

'You want your man jailed or killed on the orders of Barnaby Lant?' Vickers had asked.

Of course she didn't. Her lot would then become completely untenable. A woman left alone without money, family or position, and thus obliged to support herself, had few recourses in frontier places. A hasty remarriage or prostitution were highest on the short list of options.

Consequently, Liberty had schooled herself to put aside repugnance and gone along with a scheme to buy Vickers' silence. Tom had had only one thing worth a damn to the man they sometimes called Dirty Dan — her pretty, still youthful body. As payoff, she'd complied with an arrangement that she should be available to Vickers. Tolliver plainly saw this as no great loss to him.

Liberty had thought she could deal with the distasteful situation. Tom Tolliver had already fouled up her life. She didn't feel that she belonged to him

11

or anybody. And as a rancher's wife, she'd had practice rebuffing the average range Romeos.

But now, though steeled and stoic, she was beginning to wonder. It was difficult to overcome her instinctive horror of the practices that appealed to the man who wore the sheriff's badge.

'Show some keenness, bitch!' Vickers growled.

He clasped her head more brutally, twisting the hair at the back and bringing her closer. She had in front of her eyes only a belly white as a slug's.

A kind of panic gripped her when her throat filled. It became necessary for her to swallow rapidly and without reserve before she gagged or suffocated.

Maybe she should try to ask if he'd let her drink more of the rotgut liquor from the two-gallon stoneware whiskey jug that stood on the floor. He'd forced her to drink so much of the stuff already that her head was swimming. With more, could she make herself senseless? Would it help if she didn't know what he did to her?

But Vickers' desires were turning in another direction. He pulled her up urgently and threw her down, gasping for breath, on her back on the rope bed. Stains on the straw-filled tick and a stale-sweat smell suggested it had served in similar situations before.

He pushed her knees up and apart, forcing them high and wide, curving her body, bending it to his will. She stiffened, wishing to put this part of her life behind her as quickly as she could. Surely Dirty Dan would soon tire of her impassive resignation. After this one weekend he would move on to fresh spoils, as everyone except his wife knew to be his wont.

Within minutes, he was altogether ready again. She felt his bare, hairy legs against her inner thighs. He rammed. She groaned, feeling nothing except stabbing pain.

★　★　★

Crouched by the window, Crazy Bob McGill saw the back of a woman on her knees before Dan Vickers. She was completely naked; Vickers had his pants off and his suit coat was on a wall peg, the five-pointed, nickel-plated law badge pinned to the lapel. McGill couldn't remember the time he'd last seen a woman in a state of nature. It would have had to have been his long-departed wife.

His heart took on the weight of a lump of cold lead.

The shocking part wasn't the young woman's nakedness, or what she was doing to Vickers, but that he knew instantly who she was. His worst fear was proven — it was his own daughter, Liberty.

He cussed profanely under his breath. What the hell was she thinking of, giving herself over to the randy sheriff's cheating games? He'd never hated a man's guts more.

Of course, it was all Tom Tolliver's fault at bottom. He'd never approved of him as a son-in-law. She should never have married him. He was a no-hoper; a lazy, weak man overly fond of his own bragging voice. A bag of wind. It should have always been evident that he would be incapable of satisfying and holding a good woman.

But why this, Liberty? Why sneaking, cheap adultery in the woods with a man who, though virile in his appetites, was no more ideal than her wretched husband?

Consumed by his rage and his inability to do much about it, except maybe to create later a private chance to remonstrate with and condemn his daughter, McGill didn't hear his attacker's approach until way too late. He started to turn, a smell of stale cigar smoke coming to his nostrils and aware suddenly that he wasn't alone and his watching had been watched from a dark corner where the cabin's igneous-rock chimney abutted the wall.

'Sheriff won't like a Peeping Tom, you ol' has-been,' a voice graveled.

That was the only real warning he was given before a gun barrel cracked him across the back of the neck. He cried out in pain as he fell, his body sliding, bumpety-bump, down the log wall to slump in a heap at the bottom. Then the gun iron was applied again, harder this time, sending him into deep sleep.

* * *

'What was that? I heard a voice — some scuffling,' Liberty said.

Dan Vickers smiled thinly. 'That's no mind to you or me, whatever it is. Now you be a good girl and lie back, damnit.'

'But there could be someone outside. A snooper!'

'Forget it. Prob'ly just a rat or somesuch.'

Liberty persisted. 'What if we were found out? Your wife told? This is shameful. It's adulter — '

'No one's finding out anything! No

16

one in Redstone Gulch's gonna dare open his mouth. See?'

He slapped her face lightly.

Flinching, she fell back into the position he wanted but had the spirit to mumble, 'Maybe you should go look.'

'You think a sheriff should be poking his nose into everything?' he snarled. 'Well, it ain't so, ma'am — I'm doing all the poking I want already, see? So shuddup and bear up!'

The sounds outside had stopped as quickly as they'd begun. The revulsion of what was happening to her made it impossible to think straight. She could produce no further means to distract him from having his way.

Vickers reached down and hooked his thumb into the ear of the whiskey jug and tilted it on a hairy forearm. He took a deep swallow and smacked his lips in satisfaction.

'Ahh!' He thrust the jar toward her. 'More?'

She turned her head away dumbly, pressing her lips together. Her head was swimming from the raw liquor she'd already been obliged to swallow. Surely he'd done his worst. How would it help if she got drunk and senseless now?

Vickers laughed thickly. 'Suit yourself, woman. We've just started, mind. Thought you might've wanted a bracer for a night of it.'

2

Buzzards over the Range

Joshua Dillard had no particular taste for accommodating the whims of the rich and powerful, but he was never too stubborn to turn away an assignment promising money that would keep him better than the bums who rode and scavenged from boxcars.

The tone of Barnaby Lant's letter suggested to Joshua that the cattleman was an obnoxious person. It was presumptuous, referring to work done for various cattlemen's associations by the Pinkerton Detective Agency, and suggesting that as a 'defrocked' member of that organization, with a rep for toughness and 'known to be possessed of finances commonly in a parlous state', Mr Dillard would leap to Lant's bidding.

In short, Lant came across as a pompous fool. But Joshua didn't care to contradict anyone who enclosed a letter of credit to cover his travel expenses to Montana. Also outlined was a situation that implied some thieving, trespassing curly wolves were at work and their activities could lead to a range war.

Interesting, Joshua thought, and deserving of his attention though maybe not entirely on Lant's account.

Joshua hated lawbreakers. Since the killing of his wife by outlaws in San Antonio, his mission in life had been to eliminate as many of the breed as semi-lawfully possible. He knew range wars attracted hardcases and malefactors who set little value on others' lives. Invariably, they hurt the innocent and the little people while the bigger players got off scot-free once calm was restored and territory reallocated, legally or illegally.

So sure, Joshua would go look into what was happening in the Redstone Gulch country . . . and he'd let this

Lant pay the bills. No problem with that! Seemed like the cow-country company owner was laying his money on the barrel-head. He wasted no time in visiting the bank and converting the Flying L Ranch letter of credit into green, folding money.

As with many of his doings, Joshua's approach was unconventional and tolerable circumspect. He didn't report directly to his hirer — to whom he'd wired acceptance — but stopped off in the last town before Redstone Gulch and made discreet, preliminary inquiries.

From these, Joshua learned it was round-up time. He quickly figured one place he might get a fuller, unprejudiced picture would be at the holding grounds. Accordingly, he kitted himself out with a horse and second-hand duds that included a faded, sweat-stained red shirt, a yellow bandanna, a short, washed-out denim jacket and pliable, comfortable chaps made from Angora goatskin.

He also picked a center-fire or three-quarter-rigged single-cinch Montana saddle, suggestive of a cowboy who throws a long rope then secures it with a quick dally around the horn.

He rode a rented steeldust out across the rolling waves of green and amber rangeland and came to the Flying L camp between sundown and first guard time. He looked every inch of his six-foot-plus frame like a drifter of the grub-line-riding type, traveling light without so much as a pack horse.

The boss of the round-up crew told him, 'Light down, stranger. You're jus' in time for grub. Turn your hoss into the remuda. Spend the night as you like.'

But Joshua detected he did it begrudgingly. Uneasiness was in the camp.

Joshua expected to be treated with some clabber-mouthed reserve. Cowpunchers could be a clannish lot, reluctant to speak right up to a newcomer. There were the occasional braggarts among range hands, but most of them didn't talk idly or dishonestly.

The men here had the silence of suspicion and some had the look of renegades on the dodge — gun-handling, fighting types shipped in as though in readiness for a fight. They eyed him like so many wolf-hounds.

Joshua thought he recognized one surly waddie as a felon called Tex Pynchon, reputed down in the Big Bend country to be without equal in the use of his guns. Maybe he'd seen a Pinkerton mugshot of the fellow. The agency diligently clipped every newspaper report of crime and criminals and kept folders with pictures in central files. The practice, a successful Pinkerton innovation, was being adopted by police forces.

That wasn't all Joshua noted. Against custom, reps from bordering outfits were conspicuous by their absence from the round-up camp. This reinforced the impression that good relations and fellowship were out.

Later, Joshua offered to do a shift on night guard, showing willing to earn his supper. But the ramrod, Carl Pederson, ruled that out with gruff abruptness. He let him fetch water from a creek to the mess tent for the use of the round-up cook, who was rassling a large ball of sourdough into loaves with fists that looked like they were better suited for, and practiced at, dealing punches.

'Not much harmony in this camp,' Joshua ventured as an opening conversational gambit.

The cook scowled and thumped his dough.

'No call for any, mister. From looks, yuh'd be one to go along with the argument a man's business is his own.'

Joshua didn't press it. He shrugged and moved off.

'I'll be riding on at first light. Maybe before.'

A bright-eyed young bronc-rider who'd overheard the exchange came up to him. He was an extroverted type who looked as though he might be fond of the joshing and hoorawing that was a feature of more congenial camps.

'Cookie's hotcakes ain't worth a damn,' he confided, 'but he was prob'ly taken on for other skills. An' he's right. A man travelin' light, without a packed bed horse, is figured for an outlaw on the dodge or a John Law on some kinda secret mission. Which is it, friend?'

Joshua laughed off his guesswork. 'Like Cookie says, a man's business is his own.'

'Sure, it isn't the Western way to pry,' the cowboy said.

He stuck out his hand. 'I'm Jim Stebbings. I take sides with none, but I knowed this outfit when she was a heap friendlier an' peaceable. Now there's diff'rent jaspers gettin' hired on.'

Joshua shook the offered hand. 'Do tell. The name's Joshua Dillard and this whole section's new to me. I'm some puzzled. I savvy nerves are frayed . . . '

Jim Stebbings produced the makings for brown-paper cigarettes and they lighted them up and chatted companionably.

'The buzzards are gatherin' over the range,' Jim said.

'And what might that mean?'

'It means like as not they sees somethin' dead or dyin' on the ground.'

'Sure, I know that.'

'Waal, I figger, an' they figger, it's the Flyin' L is dyin'.'

'Dying?'

'Yeah, about to turn up its toes. It began soon as Adam passed away.'

'Oh, which Adam was this?' Joshua asked, wondering if he was speaking metaphorically and that the Flying L Cattle Company had been failing for many years.

'Why the Ol' Man, o' course. Adam Lant ruled the valley. He took over an' held all the good graze. Guess he was like one o' those ol' world pirate captains, but on land. He was bandit chief, tyrant an' despot all rolled into one. He pushed most ever'body else off into the hills.'

He waved a hand airily to encompass wider terrain which Joshua had seen consisted of bleak, high, timber- and canyon-snarled badlands.

'They scratch a poor livin' in them parts, but with Barnaby Lant inheritin', they're eyin' the greener meadows, movin' stock onto 'em brazenly even. Neighbors gamble that Barnaby ain't made outa the same stuff as his pa — he don't have Ol' Adam's toughness nor vim, fer a fact. Some point out they'se only reclaimin' range they'd the use of till Adam hogged it.'

'Can't any of this be settled in law?'

Jim spread his hands. 'I ain't no attorney, friend. But if a shootin' ruckus starts, I'm quittin' certain. My advice, if yuh're here with a mind to horn in, is t' stay away!'

'Leave the pickings to those buzzards, eh? And who are the buzzards?'

'Why, the small ranchers an' riff-raff from the hills. An' the rustlers.'

Joshua's ears pricked up. This was a new angle.

'Rustlers?'

Jim nodded solemnly.

'Rough tally o' what's circled on the bed-ground is there's more'n a thousan' head o' Flyin' L beeves gone missin'. Adam gone don't mean there's been hand-shakin' and sentiment. Trouble is closin' in on all sides o' the Flyin' L.'

'So what's your boss doing about that?'

'Mr Barnaby is — 'scuse my bluntness — a sour cuss, mighty fond o' the bottle an' grouchin'. Ol' Adam would've been pawin' the dirt an' bellerin'. But Barnaby, he hates to be hurried. With his spread under siege, he's hired on hand-picked, lazy gunhawk trash; told some good beef-men past fightin' prime to roll their blankets an' quit. When the battle comes, if'n it does, is any man's guess.'

Joshua whistled.

'Who are the rustlers? The smaller ranchers and the men from the hills?'

'Mebbeso. Mebbe not. Lant don't know. Nobody knows. Ol' Adam improved his stock — good shorthorn blood in 'em, the better to live through the Montany winters.'

Joshua nodded; he'd noted this in his short time at the cow camp. The herds packing the Flying L brand were of a kind that didn't die off without barns, windbreaks and snow fences to provide the critters with shelter from the harsher blizzards. Nor did they call for the cutting of so many bales of hay for winter feed.

Jim went on, 'The smaller men are stuck with their ugly, bony longhorns. Go figger the temptations.'

Carl Pederson spotted their conflab and strode up.

'Ain't you got somethin' else to do, Stebbings? And you, mister — we don't like sticky-beaks.'

Joshua had heard enough to know that the situation was as ugly and dangerous as it had looked. No good would come from antagonizing his client's crew.

'Beg pardon, ramrod, and thank you kindly for the supper vittles. I've a notion to move on to town anyhow.

Nice evening for a ride.'

He touched his hatbrim and moved away from the mess-tent, setting course for the rope horse-corral. 'See you in Redstone Gulch sometime maybe,' he said, keeping his tone neutral but seething inwardly.

A flush stole across Pederson's grumpy face.

'Damnit, stranger! Leave when you please,' he growled. 'And be sure that corral's tied shut when you go.'

The case had more wrinkles than an old squaw, Joshua reflected. A falling-out with Barnaby Lant's crew would be unhelpful. The smart start he'd thought he was making had proved inauspicious.

With effort he assumed a mask of cold reserve and went to saddle his horse.

★   ★   ★

The light was adequate, and the road to the township of Redstone Gulch clear enough, for Joshua to ride at a comfortable gait that didn't tax his tired mount. Joshua seldom abused a horse and had no reason to do so now.

The road eventually entered the gulch that gave the town its name — a winding, notch-like break in the hills that may once have promised gold but yielded little or none. Coming to a fork where a second, descending trail joined the road at the right, from the north-west, he turned to read a board sign. Over an arrow, were the rough letters: DEVIL'S LAKE, SILVER PEAK.

Several hours had passed since he'd left the round-up camp and the moon was up lending a spooky light to the scene. He observed the fresh sign of two horses and a discarded cigar butt, fat and chewed, still faintly smoldering in the dirt.

Evidently, he wasn't the only late rider heading into town.

Joshua's horse went faster, maybe sensing the other animals, breaking from a walk into an easy lope, which Joshua didn't restrain. Rounding a bend, Joshua saw ahead two horses, one being led. The man on the back of the led horse was slumped forward over the animal's neck. From the way he sat his saddle, he didn't look fit to be riding. Maybe his wrists were tied to the horn.

A drunk being helped home late by a pal? But going into town? From where?

The leading rider, alerted by the sound of loping hoofs and a frolicsome whinny from Joshua's horse, looked over his shoulder and quickly guided his own and his companion's horse off the road.

Joshua thought little of it immediately. So a pair of late carousers didn't want to be seen in an embarrassing state of inebriation, or had been visiting an out-of-town house of ill repute. It happened.

But the pair didn't stop once they'd cleared the road, allowing Joshua passage and avoiding meeting. The lead rider spurred his big bay horse and led the other down a narrow sidetrail that went through concealing brush. Maybe it was a short-cut to town. Joshua didn't know and had no reason to test alternative routes. He was in no hurry.

But being Joshua, and an ex-Pink, his curiosity was piqued.

When he reached Redstone the town, he did a circuit of its empty, darkened streets, scanning them for evidence of the pair's arrival. He noted the locations of the key buildings. The settlement was a typical cow-town: a big mercantile store, livery barn, sheriff's office and lock-up, black-smith's forge, large saloon, two-story hotel, restaurant and several smaller businesses like a saddlery and a haberdashery.

Everything was shut up for the night, even the saloon.

A light breeze sent a discarded newspaper scuttling across the dusty main drag. Someplace, a dog sensed him and set to barking till an irritated male voice silenced it with a terse command.

He saw no trace of the pair who'd dodged him on the way in until he was back to his starting point on the outskirts. Then he spotted them.

They were outside a dilapidated, solitary frame house — little better than a shack — surrounded by a broken-down picket fence that had once been painted white, but was now mostly weather-grayed, bare timber and moldy green stains. Set back from the road, the sad-looking property was divided from it by a ditch.

Joshua drew back into the shadows of a big cottonwood.

The man on the bay, whom he'd supposed the other's pal, dismounted and cut the ropes that stopped the reeling 'drunk' slipping from the saddle. He didn't help him down. He pitched him off the horse like a sack of feed.

'You're home, Crazy Bob,' he said. 'Stay away from the lake! What Dirty

Dan does up there and to who ain't any of a loon's cut-in. No more prowling around and prying into what ain't your business, unnerstand?'

The man on the ground, who Joshua saw was bearded and elderly, groaned feebly.

'Scourings of hell, that's what you are — you an' Tolliver an' Vickers all! She's my li'le gal . . . '

The other laughed sarcastically. 'Was your little 'un, McGill — you stupid ol' has-been! Little gals ain't got the bubbies and well-rounded asses Dirty Dan has a hankering for.'

Joshua saw the supposed good Samaritan who'd proved something else thrust his booted toe viciously into the oldster's side and send him rolling into the ditch.

'Next time you won't get off so easy, mind — peeping bastard!'

The sprawling old man moaned and complained some more, incoherently. He struggled to rise out of the ditch but kept sliding back in.

His persecutor stepped up into his saddle.

Joshua decided it was time he should take a hand. He couldn't abide bullies. He rode out into the open.

'Hey! Hold up there, mister! A word . . . '

The man on the big bay gave him one swift look and dug in his spurs. 'Giddap!' he rapped.

The horse squealed and took off.

3

Shots in the Dark

Joshua gave chase, urging his steeldust after the bay. He reckoned whatever the reasons for what he'd witnessed, the man riding off lickety-split had some explaining to do.

They tore out of town. Two banners of dust whirled ghost-white in the moonlight behind them. The oldster's attacker plainly knew the terrain. He pulled the bay off the road and streaked across rough, uneven ground.

Joshua's steeldust was naturally swift, but it was a short way from played out, too. He didn't want it to stumble or take a fatal, leg-breaking fall. He eased up.

The chased man pulled ahead. Beyond range of possible identification, he turned in the saddle and raised a

37

hand-gun. Joshua saw the muzzle flash, heard the crack and felt the wind of the man's bullet as it whistled past his ducking head.

He reined up. It would be a cruel stroke of luck if he or his horse was hit by a revolver shot fired from moving horseback. In optimum circumstances, a skilled marksman with a fine weapon could hit a man at 50 yards, but firing from horseback it would be good shooting to hit a man anywhere beyond 10 yards' range.

Nonetheless, Joshua had no strong enough motive to lay his life on the line. Nor would it be fair to put at risk the game blue, a horse whose qualities he appreciated. The chance hit could happen. He let the gunfiring badman make good his retreat.

It was now well past midnight and the moon had passed its zenith and was skidding down in the sky. The horse-man was swallowed up in the darkness; sounds drifted back on the night breeze that suggested he was crashing through some brush. But silence soon fell. An owl hooted in the hills to the west. From the flats came the yip of a coyote and another's more distant answer.

Joshua pulled round the steeldust and rode back the way he had come. The old-timer in the ditch was to be considered. He'd looked in need of aid. Likely, he could answer the questions he'd wanted to put to his attacker.

★　★　★

The oldster was still stuck in the drainage ditch, crumpled and beaten. What was it the other had called him? 'Crazy Bob' and 'Mac' something . . . MacGuire? No, McGill, that was it.

Joshua took his horse across the ditch, over the rotting boards of a wooden ramp, and hitched the reins to the crooked fence. McGill was cussing weakly.

'Soon have you out of there, yessir!' Joshua said encouragingly. 'Mr McGill, wasn't it?' He went down on one knee and held out his hand. 'Here, take a hold.'

He half-hauled McGill up. His face, grizzled hair and shabby clothes were plastered with thick, slimy mud. And he was so groggy, he could barely stand.

Joshua supported and half-carried him into his wreck of a home. The place had a front parlor, a kitchen and a tiny bedroom. Everywhere seemed crowded with ancient, tobacco-brown furniture and piles of yellowing newspapers and magazines.

Joshua struck a match and lit a lamp with a smoke-tinted chimney. He inspected his battered host and found he had a lump on the back of his skull bigger than a duck's egg. It was split and bleeding. He went and found a tolerably clean cloth in the kitchen and poured water from a pitcher into a tin pan.

He carried the pan through to where McGill was seated on a dining chair. He found a spot for it on the cluttered table, pushing aside a letter half-written in a spidery hand on the top sheet of a lined, yellowing notepad. He squeezed out the cloth and began bathing the wound.

'I'd say you've been gun-whipped,' he said.

'Bent a damned gun-barrel acrost my head,' McGill muttered. He sounded aggrieved, but his outrage seemed tempered somehow by caution, as though he was scared. Or nursing a guilty secret.

Joshua said simply, gently, 'Who did it? Why?'

He also hadn't forgotten McGill had been called 'Crazy Bob' by his attacker.

His questions weren't answered.

'Damn his eyes an' ever'thing else,' McGill mumbled into bushy whiskers. 'It cuts me up. Like a dull knife blade twisted in my heart. But thank you kindly for helping a wronged and saddened man.'

Joshua was wary of pressing McGill for more information. He had a hunch, based on long experience of questioning people, that were McGill to know

Joshua was a detective, brought to Redstone Gulch by the most influential cattleman in the district, his lips would be doubly sealed.

It was evident McGill felt sorry for himself. Joshua categorized him broadly as a man in declining years and fortunes, active though slowed some by a limp that might not entirely be due to his recent mistreatment. His townsman's suit and topcoat were rumpled and threadbare as well as muddied. His hair, both head and beard, could have done with a mite of bought attention at a barbershop. Just another uncared-for old man living alone, whose woman was dead, run away, or had plain never existed in a West where some territories' female population was on a one-to-three ratio with the male.

Joshua asked, 'Don't you have someone to look after you? A wife, a daughter?'

The state of the house had already given him the negative answer, of course, but McGill might be led into providing a fuller one.

'Daughter,' he said gruffly. 'But she been married, oh, three years since.'

'Maybe she and her husband could help you. Advise you, leastwise.'

McGill shook his head. 'Not a hope in hell, feller.' Resentment made him brusque and passionate. 'I despised Tom Tolliver for his slothful ways and his brags. Howsomever, he was a favorite with the ladies and when he started calling on Liberty she was impressed, even though she knew I didn't like him. He always brought her little gew-gaws he chose outa big-city mail order catalogs and got sent him. Any girl would've been flattered and Liberty was still very young. Innocent — '

McGill choked on the word.

'Anyhow, it's no nevermind — none of anyone else's business.' He touched the bump at the back of his head. ''Sides, I don't need no nursing.'

He shifted nervously under Joshua's assessing gaze which said otherwise.

'Don't want no fuss about this, you know . . . '

Joshua regarded him sternly. 'The part I saw was unprovoked assault. You should swear out a warrant against that man. I saw a sheriff's office in town.'

McGill shook his head vigorously. 'That don't mean nothing, mister — nothing! There's no law around Redstone Gulch. The sheriff's a — a — ' Words failed him and he finished weakly, 'A political appointee, you might say. A puppet.'

'So who pulls the strings?' Joshua asked, though he thought he already knew the answer he would be given.

'If'n you plan on spending time in this neck of the woods you'll find out soon enough, stranger. This country is Lant country, and the big shot was Adam Lant. Sheriff Vickers is a Lant man, put up for and kept in office by Lant money. Adam sealed the deal by marrying his daughter to Vickers. Now, I guess it's Adam's son Barnaby who calls the tune, though he's a lesser man, and Sophie, the daughter, leads her own life and runs a haberdashery in town.'

'These Lants sound like they've got everyone treed.'

'Did have. Old Adam was hell on wheels . . . gobbled up ranch after ranch, not excepting my own small spread. He had his eyes on the whole valley. Time he was finished, he controlled just about all the rangeland worth spit within a day's ride of Redrock Gulch. Sixty thousand acres of prime graze!'

'And Sheriff Vickers is still — uh — on the Lant payroll?'

The old one's eyes blazed momentarily as though lit by remembered anger. Then his chin slumped miserably to his shirt front.

'You could put it like that, 'cept Vickers has his own irons in diff'rent kinds of fires. Meantime, it looks like trouble is brewing for Barnaby Lant other places.'

Joshua decided to say nothing of

what he knew of that side of the situation. Though McGill had told little about the assault he'd suffered, what he had told was useful.

It occurred to him that on the morrow he might profitably make contact with Sheriff Vickers. Evidently, they would be on the same side in any coming crisis. It could be a shrewd move to take Vickers into his confidence. On the one hand, it might prove as fruitless a shot in the dark as the leaden one he'd ducked. On the other, he might learn more about the cattleman who'd hired him and about his problems.

Simultaneously, it would do no harm to mention to the local peace officer the cowardly attack on an elderly citizen who it appeared was too frightened to contemplate laying his own complaint. He hoped the sheriff would have some clue to the thug's identity and would see him given his needings.

McGill offered Joshua his lumpy, spring-busted sofa for the rest of the night. Joshua thanked him but declined the offer. He found the small dwelling claustrophobic and the sofa looked far from comfortable.

Once he'd helped the old-timer safely into his bunk, Joshua left the tumble-down shack and rode the steeldust a short distance out of town to a stand of poplars by a creek. Patches of bluegrass promised to afford graze for the jaded horse. He stripped off the saddle and picketed the animal, using a lariat he'd acquired with his cowboy saddle rig.

Overhead the moon was sinking further. Long shadows were cast over the land. Soon, the moon would be gone from the sky and it would be full dark until the pale lemon light of dawn crept up over the eastern horizon.

Joshua lighted a fire just big enough to boil a billy; sipped hot, black coffee; carefully stamped out the fire.

He spread his bedroll in a spot to his liking, set his saddle for a pillow, and stretched out to rest, think and finally doze away what was left of the night.

* * *

Came the morning, Joshua returned to town where he left the steeldust at the livery barn and toted his saddle and blanket roll along to the hotel. It boasted the grand name of the Redstone House and for a cow-town was tolerably impressive.

The clerk at the desk in the carpeted lobby looked down a supercilious nose at his baggage and, after he'd signed the register, allocated him a corner room that, though spare and clean, didn't justify the hotel's rates. Still, it was better than sleeping out, gave him a neutral base and was paid for out of Barnaby Lant's travel money.

'The house rules are no drunkenness and no lady visitors in single rooms,' the clerk warned him.

Joshua washed up and left, locking the door.

His next call was at the law office. He fully intended to take the sheriff into his confidence. But he was given cause to

48

pause on the steps. A bay horse was at the tie-rail outside the office. It reminded him of the mount ridden by the man who'd dumped Crazy Bob McGill outside his shack. But the color was common enough for a horse. He went on in, ready to have his say, maybe ask some questions.

Inside, the office was the usual spartan set-up, though a deal smarter than many peace officer's premises Joshua had visited in the course of his tumultuous career.

What wasn't so smart was the gent seated, or rather slumped, behind the biggest desk with his booted feet on its remarkably empty walnut top. He was reading one of Beadle's Dime Novels, ornately titled *Deadwood Dick's Dream: or, The Rivals of the Road*.

'Are you Sheriff Vickers?' Joshua asked.

'Nope. I'm Deputy Saul Beckford,' the lounger said with an air of self-importance undermined by his slovenly posture.

'I guess I better wait for the sheriff then.'

Beckford sniggered as though this were a huge joke.

'Long wait, mister. Sheriff's outa town till Monday.'

'Oh. Then I guess he has more urgent duty than 'pears to call around here. Deadwood Dick's dream sounds kinda lazy work.'

Beckford sighed and threw down his slim, orange-covered novel.

'State your business, smart mouth.'

'None too sure I should, Deputy. I wanted a little gab with the sheriff, is all. You mightn't be competent.'

The idler was stung. He swung down his legs and started to uncoil. He was a big man with wide shoulders and ham-sized arms under a checked blue shirt over which he wore an open vest.

'Now lissen here — '

Whatever was about to transpire was forestalled by the entry from the jailhouse section to the side of the office by someone swinging a bunch of keys.

50

He'd overheard the testy exchange.

'Hold your hosses, Saul! He was jus' eggin' you on. Don't let him get your goat.'

Horses, hens and goats . . . for a moment the lingo had Joshua picturing ludicrously a straight-off-the-farm hick striding in wearing bib overalls. The reality was different.

When he swung to face him, he saw the newcomer was another big fellow, thick-set with a mean-lipped, resolute face. But more startling than any of this was that Joshua was fifty percent certain he was the man who'd dumped McGill the night before and deterred pursuit with a six-gun. Since he'd never been close enough to see the shooter's face, and this man's voice inside four solid walls had a different timbre, it was not positive identification.

Nor was he himself recognized.

'Guess you must be another o' Dan's cagey cattle-buyer friends. Or a railroad agent. The word must be getting around.'

'Dan?' Joshua asked, lost. 'Is that Sheriff Vickers?'

'You don't know? Say, who are you anyways?'

'I'm Joshua Dillard. Who are you?'

'Deputy Gustav Kurtz, sir,' the second big man said, though his 'sir' was not respectful and he looked a mite discomposed, like a man who'd spoken out of turn.

Joshua decided to probe.

'Well, Deputy Kurtz, tell me — do you know an elderly gent name of Bob McGill?'

A wariness narrowed Kurtz's eyes but only momentarily.

'Sure — Crazy Bob. What of it?'

'Thought you might've known what happened last night, when he got beat up and thrown into a ditch. And him a man past sixty years old!'

The barbed, but to a guiltless ear merely cryptic, comment scored a bull's-eye. It was Kurtz's turn to be riled, and his reaction was out of proportion to any for which Joshua was prepared.

'By God, you're right, Saul — he's got a busy lip! Figure I'll teach him to button it.'

And Kurtz launched a swinging right fist at Joshua's mouth.

4

Trail to Devil's Lake

There was nothing subtle in Gus Kurtz's way of getting things done, but Joshua was not fast enough to dodge entirely the punch his glittering eyes had telegraphed. The side of his face was smashed against his teeth and he tasted the quick presence of blood. When the likes of Kurtz's wild, big fist connected properly it would be apt to break a man's neck.

Joshua quickly stepped back, wondering how long he would be able to last. He looked for the chance an angry man always makes for his opponent.

Kurtz was a big man in good physical condition, of about thirty-five years. He came storming after Joshua like a mad bull, and threw another murderous blow at his head.

Joshua weaved under it and jabbed a fist hard into Kurtz's midriff. The wind left the deputy in a tremendous whoosh. Fixing to follow up his scant advantage, Joshua slammed a blow into the side of his jaw, which his dropped fists had left unprotected. He followed it up with a swift, poker-like left between the eyes.

Kurtz reeled back, gasping, his lips peeled back from his teeth in a snarl of hatred. Then he flew at Joshua again, propelling another punch toward Joshua's head.

Joshua nimbly dodged and took the jolting blow on his shoulder.

The pair went at it hammer and tongs, bobbing and weaving. Kurtz got in some hard, damaging strikes and Joshua, his face bloodied, began to feel the worse for wear.

But Kurtz's ferocious temper was his undoing. He began to lose again his recovered wind. A well-placed, powerful right upper-cut to his jaw and another slammed punch into his stomach were telling.

Joshua rallied. Kurtz was reeling and had given up his tactic of rushing in, bellowing, fists windmilling. Joshua was beginning to think that after a fair fight, the trading of a few more blows, he might walk out of the office with his body and dignity largely intact when out of the tail of his eye he caught movement.

Saul Beckford was choosing to take a hand. Or hands. He grabbed Joshua by his collar and an arm and dragged him backwards toward the door onto the street.

With a roar, Kurtz came after them, chopping at Joshua's head and upper body viciously. Joshua heard the thuds as though they were landing not on himself but somewhere a long way off. The scene around him span dizzyingly.

Beckford said, 'Careful, Gus. We don't know the bastard. You can't jus' kill him. Maybe he is a cattle buyer.'

Kurtz said, 'Yeah, they're good at making trouble. They buy, they sell; stay in the middle. One man's trouble is another's gain. No work, no risk. They collect the profit both ways.'

But it sounded like the words were being spoken in some vast, echoing place like a stone church in a big city.

Then Joshua thought he was flying like a bird. It seemed a long, long flight, but it couldn't have been. Fresh air and a jarring landing brought his senses out of the worst of their muddle. He was sitting in the dirt of the rutted main drag.

The deputies, who'd thrown him out the door, were dusting their hands and going back into the law office.

'Keep your nose outa what don't concern you, Dillworth or whatever your moniker was!' Beckford said over his shoulder. 'If you know what's best, you'll hightail it from Redstone pronto.'

*   *   *

Joshua picked himself up and limped back to the Redstone House, where he met a frosty reception.

'Mr Dillard!'

Joshua paused on the stair. It was the lobby clerk, distaste written large on his pale face.

'What is it?'

'The hotel is a respectable establishment with a reputation to keep up. Plainly you've been in a fight. From your gait, I'd suggest you might even be drunk despite the earliness of the hour.'

'Well, I'm not, and would it make me poison around here if I were?'

'The fighting would,' the clerk said righteously. 'The hotel don't want no ruffian for a guest.'

Joshua looked down at himself and dabbed at his bloody face with a kerchief. He was dusty and battered for a fact. He figured it would be a mistake to let on that his going-over had been at the hands of the law-office pups.

'Sure. I do look a sight,' he agreed. 'Would it help at all if I said I'm going to go find the sheriff soon as I'm washed up and wearing a clean shirt?'

'The sheriff is out of town. You'll have to report to his deputies.'

'Uh-uh.' Joshua shook his head. 'Did that. Only the top man will do.'

He turned and hobbled back down the stair and across to the desk. He felt inside his jacket and brought out his wallet from which he extracted several crisp green bills.

The clerk's frown turned to puzzlement, then to the quick appreciation that he was about to be offered money for his co-operation.

Though his fingers were stiff and the knuckles sore, Joshua made a careful show of folding the bills together into a neat, tight, small wad. It was a regrettable strain on his exchequer, but he felt that it was an investment.

'Just where does a man find Sheriff Vickers of a weekend?'

He leaned across the desk, pushing the folded bills toward the clerk's soft right hand.

The clerk hesitated but a moment. He looked about nervously, saw that they weren't observed, licked his lips and discreetly covered the money with his palm.

'Devil's Lake,' he murmured. 'It's an open secret around Redstone anyways. Vickers goes there for the — um — fishing.'

'Thank you kindly,' Joshua said. 'I'll ride up to the lake directly.'

'It might not be a good idea,' the clerk said impulsively.

'Why not?'

The clerk shrugged, at a seeming loss for words. Maybe he feared Joshua would want his money back.

'The sheriff values his privacy there.'

'Oh, I don't think he'll mind my calling. The sheriff and I have interests in common.'

The clerk dropped his eyes from Joshua's searching gaze and gulped.

'If you say so, Mr Dillard, but I wouldn't want this to backfire. I'd prefer it if you didn't mention me or the hotel as your source of information.'

Joshua reassured him, 'Consider it

your right to be an anonymous informant.'

★ ★ ★

Joshua had much to think about now he was away from Redstone Gulch with the open trail ahead of him and the sun climbing into a blue sky.

He should have had that invigorating feeling of escape and freedom which accompanies a ride by road on a fine morning. But his misgivings about accepting Barnaby Lant's money, and thereby committing himself to investigating the problems faced by the Flying L Cattle Company, were deepening.

He'd found Lant's round-up camp crewed in part by a hard-bitten, tough-as-boots bunch, some of whom were wanted men in other states and territories. Maybe Lant had good reasons for this, but if so they were facets of a policy he'd neglected to mention in his correspondence.

Joshua had also learned, albeit only

as hearsay, that the local sheriff, Dan Vickers, was part of the Lant faction. Vickers was, therefore, to be presumed an ally. But his deputies could beat up an old man and a stranger who challenged them about it. Besides which, the notion of a 'bought' peace officer conflicted with his principles.

A lawman was as prey to temptation as anybody else. Experience had taught him men wearing tin badges committed the same crimes as other men; some maintained that in the West their rate of offending was no less. The lawman had to be granted power in order to be useful in his job, but power was a great corrupter.

Gus Kurtz had brought back Crazy Bob McGill to town, unconscious, via the trail to Devil's Lake, where Vickers was spending his weekend.

Questions arose in Joshua's mind and he wanted them cleared up before he reported to the Flying L headquarters. The primary question was gallingly familiar. Had fate dealt him his usual losing hand? He couldn't get to the lake — and the lawman he reckoned would provide the answer — fast enough.

It was a sad truth that Joshua was typically muddling through an affair that had quickly lost the promise of making him clean and tolerably easy money. In part, he'd left the Pinkerton agency and become a freelance because of his inability to sell his labor for causes in which he didn't believe; to put aside his own code and produce the results required by a paymaster.

He hated injustice, but all too often it coincided with the interests of the rich and powerful. He could never forget that his wife, the light of his life, had been gunned down by a gang of hardcases in San Antonio on the strength of his allegiance to employers who in return had refused to sanction the violent methods and recklessness to which her death had inclined him.

How, then, could he now sell his services to another outfit for which he had no real sympathy?

Joshua had been in the territory of Montana before, yet not this part of it. His most recent visit had taken him to the mining town of Butte, but hereabouts stock-raising was the predominant activity.

Nelson Story, a cattleman, had driven the first herd of a thousand longhorns up the Texas Trail to the Yellowstone Valley in 1866, inspiring a significant industry. The western valleys had soon been crowded with herds which met the demands of the mining camps for beef. After the Piegan massacre by a United States Army cavalry command in 1870, the stockmen had also moved onto the vast plains ranges east of the mountains.

The Lant family had claimed its share of the cow-country action, based around its home ranch, the Flying L.

Joshua took the left fork to the lake, and came to the timbered, less-traveled section. It was beautiful, wild country of a kind he liked with sun-dappled, chuckling streams and deer trails that led off through the trees.

Because it was not a main highway, recent tracks were considerably fewer. Joshua soon became aware of a fresh set of ruts and hoofprints. They suggested to his expert eye that someone was on the same trail not so far ahead of him — riding a furiously and dangerously driven buggy.

The ruts frequently swerved off the roadway into the rough grass and softer going at its edges. Twigs of roadside scrub and trees were broken and sometimes crushed, the new fractures showing white. At corners, the buggy wheels had slewed. Where the road rounded a basaltic boulder, scrapings of black paint had been left on the rock.

Intrigued, Joshua urged the steeldust into a gallop, but all the while keeping his eyes skinned for hazards. The trail was not in good repair and he could ill-afford to court disaster of the kind to which the foolhardy buggy driver seemed oblivious.

He knew he was gaining ground on

the rig ahead of him when he could smell, strong as smoke, the dust left in its trail and hanging in visible clouds in the dense, surrounding brush.

The next sign of recent hell-bent passage added to the small sum of his knowledge and told a tale that startled him.

Caught up in the growth of brambles and dwarf spruce that grew in the shadows of the great pines at the trail's edge was a fashionable lady's parasol. It didn't look as though it had been there more than minutes. A broken metal spoke poked through a rip in one panel of the bright-green, tasseled silk cover. The shaft, some thirty inches in length, had an expensive ivory handle.

Joshua's puzzlement deepened. My God! Could it be a woman riding the forest trail so recklessly?

A low pine limb, overhanging the trail, might easily have snagged the parasol and sent it flying out of an owner's hand, especially if she was also trying to manipulate the lines of a conveyance driven helter-skelter.

Seconds later, above the swift clip of his own horse's hoofs, Joshua heard a sudden squeal of equine distress that turned and sickened his stomach. It told him his chase was about to end.

Rounding a bend, he came across the scene of the wreck. A glance was enough to tell him what had happened. Inevitably, the buggy's journey had ended prematurely in tragedy.

The horse, a gray mare, was down, wallowing in the dust and the forest detritus at the trailside, bawling and panic-stricken. The capsized buggy to which it was hitched had ended up in the underbrush against a massive tree bole. A smashed offside wheel was still slowly spinning. Joshua saw immediately that although the horse's legs were thrashing wildly, it couldn't rise and the left foreleg was broken.

Back a piece, a well-dressed lady in green silk was also on the ground, but in the middle of the trail. With her crumpled dress and petticoats thrown up above her knees, she looked like a drunk or a high-class whore sleeping off exhaustion, forgetful of decorum and where she was.

Joshua's horse galloped past her and came to a halt with a few stiff-legged plunges when Joshua hauled back on the reins. Joshua slipped from the saddle and turned his first attention to the stricken horse.

He did what he had to do. He drew his Peacemaker and shot the hapless mare through the head. The bullet drilled an instantly effective .45 caliber hole between the wide staring eyes. The squealing ended in a rasping snort. The legs and struggling body made a few more pathetic jerks and stilled.

Joshua walked back to the woman, the smoking gun hanging loosely at his side.

5

Wife on the Warpath

At the cabin on the shore of Devil's Lake, Liberty Tolliver had endured a sleepless and shattering night. Dan Vickers had imposed upon her till she was brought to the point of prostration — a condition into which he himself had lapsed only at first light. Now, with dust motes dancing in the sunlight shafting through the cabin's windows, he was snoring in a surfeit of the pleasures wrung from her sore and soiled body.

She felt drained of strength and emotion. The notion of her times was that sex was animal. The feminists campaigned not for women's rights to freer sexual expression but that men should have theirs reduced. The Victorian feminist, fearing pregnancy, prostitution, disease and debility, believed she was her own savior from the slut within herself. The feminist saw it as her mission to deny troublesome sex. Thus she rescued herself from the fate of the whore and the street walker driven by awakened and inconvenient appetites.

Because of the taboo that sexual matters were unmentionable in public, Liberty knew she would never obtain redress for the long night's debauch, just as she had known prior protest and resistance were useless.

Dirty Dan Vickers had made every possible ingress. Liberty shuddered. She knew he would repeat his indulgence, over and over. There would be no escape from his torment until he found novelty elsewhere.

But for now he slept, sated.

Fleeing the cabin was not worth consideration — where could she go? — but she did have the chance to clean herself up, which might help salvage some small part of her battered self-respect.

Silently, she rose and dragged a zinc bathtub from the cabin out back. She also found a once-white towel; though grayish it would serve. She filled the tub from the sun-warmed barrel that collected the rain from the roof.

She climbed in, intending to soak off and wash away the discomfort and signs of the night's abuse. The task was barely begun when she became aware that her preparations had masked the sounds of an arriving audience.

Her ablutions were being watched by a lone man seated on a black gelding. He was dark-haired, middle-aged, long-legged, long-armed, deep-chested and pugnaciously browed. He was also humorless. She recognized him instantly.

He was Barnaby Lant, whose inheritance was the largest cattle spread in the Redstone Gulch country. His lack of amusement didn't prevent him taking a long and good look at her, though his widened eyes remained habitually dull. He leered and grunted. It was unclear whether he approved or disapproved of what he surveyed comprehensively in a kind of morbid fascination.

'So you're Dirty Dan's latest flame, are you?' he said moodily. 'And that no-account Tom Tolliver's woman unless I miss my guess . . . which I could, not having had the privilege o' seeing you naked as a jaybird before. But I think not. Your points of appeal look kinda diff'rent from Vickers' usual run of honky-tonk gals.'

Liberty face went crimson-hot and she didn't know where to put her hands to best effect.

* * *

Joshua thrust the Peacemaker back into its holster and knelt beside the stunned woman lying in the dust of the narrow roadway.

A faint, heady perfume tickled his nostrils.

She was a brunette of about five-and-thirty, a townswoman with gloved hands and smooth, olive-colored skin that had never suffered the ravages of the elements. A nose of Grecian cast gave her a haughty look even in repose. Her glossy hair was drawn back from her face in a bun.

Propriety denied Joshua a full examination, but although she had a few conspicuous bruises, she didn't appear to have suffered broken limbs. The day was growing hot and breathless and might have contributed to her accident and her faint.

Joshua fetched the canteen slung from his saddle and dashed the pale face with water. She came out of her insensibility quickly and opened large, full dark eyes. She spluttered.

'Wh-who are you? What in God's name do you think you're doing?'

'Helping you, ma'am. You wrecked your buggy. I think you were thrown and knocked senseless.'

'That fool mare! She ran the buggy off the road and over a rock. I must have swooned dead away is all.' She touched her head. 'My hat! Where is my beautiful hat?'

Her manner and reactions irritated Joshua mightily, but given her spill, he was prepared to make concessions. Maybe she didn't really know what she was saying. Maybe she was suffering from shock or concussion.

'Your hat might have fallen off in the buggy,' he said tentatively. 'You were driving that rig at one hell of a speed. Downright foolhardy!'

While he was speaking, the brunette sat up and he helped her to her feet, but she brushed his hand off her arm.

'Don't be impertinent, sir! I was in a justifiable hurry.'

She ignored the dead horse and went straight to the buggy, and around to its far side.

Joshua was astonished. If she'd been a man, he might have felt moved to knock her teeth down her throat. But he held his rising temper over her high-handed attitude. Maybe she just might be able to explain credibly and civilly her wild ride in the buggy.

He watched incredulously as she re-appeared within moments clutching a showy, plumed hat and a reticule.

'You were right, Mr — ?'

'Joshua Dillard is my name. And yours?'

'I'm Mrs Sophie Vickers, wife of the Sheriff of Redstone County and proprietor of the Redstone Haberdashery Emporium.'

Joshua inclined his head and touched his hatbrim.

'If you'll forgive my continuing impertinence, why were you in such an all-fired rush?'

'It's confoundedly rude of you to ask a lady's private business, Mr Dillard, but I had — *have* — good reason. I am wronged! Most shamefully wronged . . .'

'How so, ma'am?'

Her dark eyes flashed and her bosom heaved. 'I'm a woman deceived! I will have my revenge!'

Joshua said doubtfully, 'You will?'

For answer she dipped her hand into

her reticule and produced a derringer pistol. Joshua recognized it as being of the Remington pattern, a kind which many women in the more unruly Western towns kept for defense. The small, two-shot weapon was easily concealed in a purse or even a stocking top.

Sophie flourished the pistol dramatically.

'I'm going to Devil's Lake to have it out with my cheating husband and his whore!'

''Cept your buggy is wrecked and your horse dead,' Joshua reminded her. He also reflected silently that her stated mission with a pepperbox pistol was apt to become an unwanted interruption to his own business.

'I take it you have good evidence for your scandalous charges,' he said.

Triumphantly, she dug again into her reticule and produced a sheet of paper. She shook out the folds and flourished this, too, with equal drama.

'It's all here!'

Joshua took the paper and scanned it. He saw it was an unsigned letter accusing in spidery handwriting that '*your man Dan Vickers is fornicating with Mrs Liberty Tolliver up at the Devil's Lake . . . I seen it with my own eyes*'.

Despite its anonymity, Joshua thought he knew who had written it. The paper was lined and yellowed by light and age at the edges. He'd seen a tablet of the same poor-quality stock just recently — at the house of Crazy Bob McGill!

'Wouldn't it be better to let the law take its course?' he suggested tentatively.

'Dan Vickers *is* the law,' Sophie stormed scornfully. 'He was put in place by my father's money to do his will and I was part of the deal. Well, the deal's off!'

Joshua pondered on the complications the accusation posed. The beaten oldster McGill had told him a no-good by the name of Tom Tolliver was the man his daughter, Liberty, had married. Various facts were starting to fit together to make a sequence, an unpleasant sense.

He began to murmur, 'You know, this is just a poison-pen lett — '

But all at once, he realized that while he was standing lost in contemplation, he'd also been left alone. His eyes lifted from the mischievous paper. When he saw what was going on, he crumpled the letter and thrust it into his pocket. He rushed forward.

Sophie Vickers had run to his horse, hiked up her skirts and, left foot in stirrup, was about to swing into the saddle.

'Hey! You can't take that horse!' he hollered.

Only an outburst of mocking laughter floated back.

Joshua's face went gaunt and pale with anger. The damned, hoity-toity madam with her pocket pistol and troublemaking letter was figuring to leave him stranded in the middle of nowhere . . .

★ ★ ★

What was worse? To be an unfaithful wife, or for it to be revealed to a third party? Liberty's embarrassment at being discovered by the sour but prominent Barnaby Lant — naked in a private setting where she had no right to be — wasn't alleviated when his leer turned to a sneer and he turned his attention to the cabin.

He bawled, 'Dan Vickers! You in there? Show your blasted hide — it's your'n I want to see, not your fallen woman's!'

Liberty had yet other, equally strong causes for alarm. Had Lant found out about her husband's altering of Flying L brands? Had he come here to prefer charges and press for her husband's head as an example to the foothills roughnecks said to be challenging his supremacy?

If so, her shameful sacrifice as the price for Dan Vickers' inaction had been in vain.

Lant dismounted and shambled up to the cabin door. His movements in boots designed for the stirrup were ungainly and stiff. He was like a sullen ape.

Vickers emerged, tucking his white silk shirt into his hastily donned pants.

'Why, Barnaby — what brings you up here?'

'I've lost another herd! A full hundred head this time. What are you doing about it?' Lant droned. 'Ain't you still the official law in this bailiwick?'

'Sure, Barnaby.'

'Rustlers are robbing the Flying L blind. It's high time you turned a hand to it — ' he cast a brief eye at Liberty, his lip curling ' — in lieu o' turning it in other places . . . Catch 'em! Shoot 'em! Hang 'em!'

'It'd prob'ly need a posse.'

'Then raise one. You've gotten the powers for that as sheriff, Vickers, and the Flying L expects results. It's your duty to get 'em. Open war is threatening.'

Liberty shrank down into the tub, trying to hide herself, and listened.

80

Vickers said apologetically, 'It ain't like the rustlers got some robbers' roost in the hills that we could raid. They're probably envious neighbors, Barnaby. Your pa took many thousand acres of virgin grassland and the Flying L has the fattest cows in consequence.'

Lant remained belligerent. He looked down his nose, unconvinced.

'But they're stealing my beef! Where are they hiding or selling it? Find out that, pronto!'

'Must be the railroad camps, Barnaby. I ain't got the jurisdiction, you know that. Those rag-tag places come and they go, a law unto theirselves. But you've ridden a piece. Come inside and set a while and we'll study on our options. I've got an unopened bottle of the finest imported whiskey. For special visitors you 'preciate, I'm sure.'

They went inside.

Vickers was a plausible rogue, Liberty had to admit. No cattle-country peace officer could do much to contain the anarchy of the ever-shifting, roaring railroad campsites. Just as they had hangers-on in the form of saloonmen and whoremongers operating tawdry businesses out of tents for the entertainment of burly laborers of all races, so they had their own butchers. They paid bags of hard cash for stock and slaughtered to feed voracious, work-sharpened appetites without asking questions.

The buffalo hunters were gone, the great herds vanished with them. But still the railroad enterprises had pushed their way out of the Dakotas and were continuing a slow crawl across the territory. The wide-open, brawling camps were everywhere, some of them many miles ahead of the track-laying crews and the work trains. They provided a ready market for unscrupulous providers of goods, services and meat.

Vickers wouldn't find it hard to produce excuses for doing nothing about Lant's problems which, as canny folks savvied, boiled down really to the fact that he was a mere shadow of his near-legendary father, Old Adam.

Liberty stepped out of the tub and put the towel around her body. Though it was gray and had a clinging, stale odor, the towel afforded a welcome modicum of modesty.

She crept up closer to the cabin and stood beneath the window. Inside, Lant was continuing to rumble and grumble, his speech now slightly slurred by the liquor.

'There will be range war, I declare. If you do nothing, I will, and I'll have your badge to boot. I've drawn Lant money from the bank to hire on pistol talent.'

'You sure that was wise, Barnaby?' Vickers asked gently, seeking to calm the big man.

The sheriff's strategy of plying Lant with fine whiskey sounded like it had been a mistake. Lant's constitution was such that he couldn't hold his liquor. It had produced the effect of making him more morose, and vindictive.

'I aim to set a range detective loose to get to the bottom of who's organizing the raids on the Flying L,' he disclosed. 'This snooper's a feller with a gun rep and a record for results. They say he's ruthless in cleaning up owlhoots and the scum who succor them.'

Vickers said cagily, 'Aw, these mercenaries are jus' soldiers-of-fortune, Barnaby. Maybe you should save your pa's money for something better. Your detective's prob'ly a bounty hunter who'll do no more'n raise dust and hell.'

The suggestion did nothing to sweeten the ponderous Lant's black mood.

'He'll raise something more'n a skirt, which is 'bout all I ever hear of you raising, Dan Vickers! That Liberty Tolliver out there — it'd be a fair assumption her stony-broke husband could be in cahoots with the rabble outfits from the badlands encroaching on my range. You looked into that?'

This for Liberty — and doubtless Vickers — was sailing frighteningly close to the truth.

Vickers sought to placate the cattle-man; to distract him. The line of appeasement he took filled Liberty with chilling new horror.

'Why, sure, Barnaby. I did consider Tolliver and his friends might've stolen a cow or two. But listen here, haven't I got a fine little heifer of Tolliver's own here for compensation? She's no drudge and she'll do anything I tell her. Anything . . . '

Liberty was shocked into raising her head and daring to peer in at the window. Neither man, fortunately, was facing it. She saw the randy sheriff crudely nudge the half-drunk Lant and wink.

'Now how about it, Barnaby? Let's say you do what I do: put your cares aside, enjoy yourself with some of life's bonuses. Let's get that handsome Tolliver woman in here. We'll learn her how to ride double — that's a trick her dolt of a husband'll never've dreamed of!'

6

Hornets' Nest

Joshua's rented steeldust was untried in the matter of women's laughter and flapping skirts, either singly or together. When Sophie Vickers tried to mount, mocking Joshua with her audible amusement, the horse was spooked and moved round.

The woman's foot slipped from the stirrup. She hauled on the reins. The horse whinnied and tossed its head.

The chance was all Joshua needed. Before Sophie's foot was back in the stirrup to make a second attempt, he was upon her, pulling her away from the sidestepping steeldust.

Spitting an unladylike cuss word, Sophie swung her reticule. Weighted with the eleven ounces of nickel plated steel that was was the hideout gun, it met Joshua's left ear with bruising impact. She broke away.

'Hey, that does it, hellcat!' Joshua said.

Too much was at stake to play the gentleman any longer. He reached for her again . . . and again she squirmed out of his grabbing hands and backed away. This time she fished the short-barreled derringer out of the bag and pointed it, seemingly with every intention of firing.

Joshua had heard it claimed that the .41 caliber rimfire bullet from a Remington double derringer moved only slowly — at about 425 feet per second — that sometimes it didn't even penetrate a targeted victim's clothing. And Sophie's gun sure had an ornamental look, with pearl grips instead of the more common hard rubber. But Joshua wasn't prepared to gamble its load wouldn't be fatal at close quarters.

He threw himself onto Sophie bodily, seizing her gun wrist and bearing her to the ground. She howled at him, screaming filth about his parentage he'd thought he'd only ever hear in the roughest saloon.

The derringer went off with a loud crack and the slug whizzed up and away into the dark-green canopy of the overhanging trees. Each of the gun's two barrels held one round, and a cam on the hammer alternated between top and bottom barrels.

Joshua wasn't going to let the hammer drop a second time. He twisted Sophie's wrist brutally with both his hands till the smoking sneak pistol was relinquished and she was brought under his control.

Cusses turned to sobs.

'Bastard! Give me back my pistol! I need it. I'm going to shoot Liberty Tolliver and my cheating husband both, do you hear?'

Joshua pocketed the gun and turned hard blue eyes on the bitter woman.

'I hear you, but I'll keep the gun. I know your husband's the sheriff — I figure to visit with him myself — but

I've heard about Mrs Tolliver only from her elderly father, Robert McGill.'

'Huh, that man is senile — a soft-brain! They call him Crazy Bob. What would he know about his daughter's goings-on? She lets the townspeople think butter wouldn't melt in her mouth, but it seems she's a snake in the grass! If the letter's true, and I find her at Daniel's cabin, I won't need my gun. I'll scratch her eyes out!'

Joshua didn't consider it wise to tell her he strongly suspected Liberty Tolliver's pa was the author of the anonymous letter. He wondered if Crazy Bob had stopped to think through its possible repercussions.

Maybe he, Joshua, was guilty of a dereliction of duty in not caring longer for the injured, solitary oldster. The crack on his head may have left him concussed, muddled in his thinking as well as sore. Should he have insisted on taking him to a doctor, assuming Redstone had one?

'Well, I don't think it would be a

good notion for you to attack anyone,' he told Sophie diplomatically. 'We'll ride my horse double to Devil's Lake like sensible people and see what we find. Your husband's an elected officer of the law and I presume a man of standing in the community.'

Sophie was scornful.

'Tchah! Daniel Vickers achieved his status courtesy of my departed father Adam Lant's influence and money. Pa virtually arranged that I should be wedded to him. It was a marriage of convenience. A steady income from the collection of county fees and taxes for Daniel; the official law in the family, and therefore in his pocket, for my dear, domineering father.'

Joshua could easily appreciate how it might have served the ambitious stockman's interests to have the sheriff as a family member as he'd expanded his cattle empire. In his time with the Pinkertons, Joshua had seen the machinations of the cattle raisers' associations and their 'barons' in acquiring powers of dubious legality, even bids to take control of territorial legislatures. Why not a bought sheriff?

Overpowered, and the fangs that were her derringer pistol drawn, the bitter Sophie was obliged to fall in with Joshua's proposal. Under a double load, the steeldust continued on the trail to Devil's Lake.

The stiff language of Sophie Vickers' body in the saddle in front of him conveyed to Joshua the message she was no longer in a blind and impelling rage. But she seethed quietly.

* * *

When Gus Kurtz looked out the window of the sheriff's office in Redstone and saw his boss's wife leaving town in a buggy he knew she must have hired from the livery barn, he sized up the unusual happening and did what he thought would be best.

'Hold the fort, Saul,' the beefy deputy told his colleague Beckford.

'Dirty Dan's missus is going buggy riding on her lonesome, and she looks to be in a damn' hurry. If she's taken it into her dumb head to go calling on her philandering spouse, it could cause trouble for everyone.'

He finished what he was doing in the sheriff's office, and went out to unhitch his bay. He tightened the saddle, stepped into it and followed in Sophie Vickers' tracks.

His thoughts were grim. Dirty Dan was jeopardizing a sweet little racket with his womanizing. Already he'd been obliged to take care of his new lady's nosey father and a grub-line rider who'd interfered in his accomplishment of the chore. Now it looked like Dan's wife might be on the same scent.

In the event, Kurtz was further delayed, and it was all down to Sophie Vickers' haste.

He was hailed by a clerk from the mercantile, who told him the home behind Vickers' haberdashery store had caught fire. Investigation proved the report alarmist. Imminent disaster was not about to befall the township, though plenty of smoke poured from a window and through the door when they forced entry.

It transpired that before leaving Sophie had emptied the ash from the cast-iron box stove. This was a twice-daily chore for householders.

The clerk, who had eight children, said in a tone of self-congratulation, 'My wife spends hours every day sifting ashes, fetching the wood, lighting the fire, adjusting the damper and rubbing our stove with thick black wax to keep it from rusting.'

Kurtz couldn't see the uppity Sophie Vickers, nee Lant, expending such effort on a stove.

In fact, in her haste, Sophie had been careless. She'd spilled hot embers on a piece of carpet which had singed and smoldered, producing the copious and disturbing quantities of smoke.

The incipient house fire was quickly stamped out.

The clerk looked to assign blame for the fuss he'd raised.

'Who can find a virtuous woman?' he quoted piously. 'For her price is far above rubies.'

Gus Kurtz just cursed.

Later, the anger roiled up inside Kurtz again when he saw Sophie Vickers' buggy tracks did, in fact, lead to the Devil's Lake trail. How come she was moving so carelessly and fast? He dug spurs into the bay. The road didn't carry much traffic. Dare he stop Sophie? What could he say that would turn her back from Vickers' hang-out?

Fresh sign of another rider, and his growing uncertainty, soon gave him cause to slacken his pace. He was obliged to reconsider his planned intervention.

Who was the other rider? Had he got it wrong that Sophie was riding out to surprise her husband?

It was while reflecting that he heard a woman's indignant screams followed by a single crack of pistol fire.

'What the hell — ?'

Into Kurtz's confused but crafty mind crept the notion that though he was right on Sophie's tail he'd be best advised to proceed with some caution. He remembered then the stranger who'd come calling for Dan Vickers.

Somehow, the man's unheralded arrival took on a fresh aspect in the light of the latest, mysterious developments. He and Saul might have been over-hasty, rash even, in throwing him out with a warning and orders to ride. Dan Vickers might not be glad to hear about it. If the stranger was mixed up in the ruckus uptrail, possibly it hadn't been the smartest play.

Could be the salty visitor had been a glory-hunting, private lawdog nosing around, Kurtz thought, his piggish eyes narrowing. Range detectives were known to hang up some mighty clever bluffs.

Further unease revolved around Dirty Dan's choice of company at the cabin. Liberty Tolliver had already put him to the bother of quietening Crazy

Bob. She was a different proposition from the changing parade of upstairs girls Vickers usually took to his lakeside love nest.

* * *

That moment, arriving at Vickers' cabin, Joshua Dillard was finding a hornets' nest rather than a love nest. Familiar though he was at sticking his head into the former, the female shrieks and protests from the small, log-built hang-out made his blood run hot with anger. It didn't help any that they were punctuated with male guffaws and a loud 'oh yeah' of satisfaction.

'It's true — she's there!' Sophie yelled in his ear. 'That's Liberty Tolliver's voice, I'd swear.'

'Shut up, get down and stay with the horse!' Joshua said. His voice, face and eyes were hard, bleak, brooking no argument.

They dismounted and Joshua stormed the cabin.

Drawing his Peacemaker, he kicked open the door of the cabin and surged through. He took in the scene in one swift glance.

Three pairs of eyes swiveled to him in sudden silence. The two men present were caught red-handed, pawing over a helpless young woman like a pair of hogs.

'Enough! Get away from that woman!' Joshua rapped. 'Fast! The pair of you!'

'Who the hell are you?' the thicker-set man asked.

'No friend of low-down yellow bellies. I ought to gut-shoot 'em while you got 'em on show! Don't take much courage to go two against one woman who's unwilling.'

'She was flaunting herself naked outside in the yard. This is her needings — nothing bad. The place's a ten-mile jaunt from town. Sluts are apt to get their comeuppance, holing up private with a married gent.'

The man's speech was slurred and he had the high color of someone with too much drink in him. Whether that made him more dangerous or less, Joshua could hazard no guess.

'Says you! I figure you're the breed that likes to kick other people around. It won't work with me. I say you're cheap and gutless!'

The second man was more composed.

'You got plenty guts your ownself, I see, hiding behind a gun. Very brave.'

Joshua didn't like his sarcasm one bit. This, he figured, was Dan Vickers. From what he was wearing of his clothes, and what was scattered around, he placed him, like his wife, as a vain individual of the type generally referred to as a dude in Western towns.

'I don't need a gun. And I haven't started yet. Get up!'

Vickers said, 'Listen, fiddlefoot, you've got this all wrong. It ain't what you think. I'm the Redstone County Sheriff.'

'Figured that. I came here to see you. Well, I seen you, bully-boy.'

'A smart-aleck as well as brave, huh?'

The bigger, quieter man of the pair spoke again, delivering his words ponderously.

'Let's quit the bickering, gents. I'm Barnaby Lant, boss of the Flying L. In case you don't know, stranger — and it's plain you don't — that makes me the top dog in this section. Buck me and you'll regret it. I've hired a tough crew and I got a range dick with a damn' mean gun rep heading for Montany momentarily. Believe me — anyone goes up against me or the Flying L outfit from now on is gonna get cut down mighty quick!'

Joshua Dillard felt the beginnings of an inner groan. The situation had an all-too-familiar ring. Figuratively, he'd shot himself in the foot yet again. Another mission, another promisingly lucrative assignment, was slipping out of his grasp.

All too often this was the way it panned out. The dinero was right; the job took his fancy. Then came the crunch, the turning point where everything boiled down into a bigger, more stinking mess than sonofabitch stew, and the prospect of reward and a stablizing of his finances abruptly vanished into thin air.

But Joshua didn't wrestle long with the dilemma this time. So what if he was back to being broke? He wasn't going to cheat himself of the pleasure of disabusing Barnaby Lant.

'Reckon not, Mr Lant. Maybe I play it wrong, but I live straight. See, sir, I am your Joshua Dillard and no man buys my integrity. Nor any excuse for a man.'

Lant gave a bear-like growl. 'You're Dillard?'

'Sure,' Joshua said bleakly. 'Isn't that what I said?'

Lant was no fast thinker, but once the truth dawned he visibly reached a decision.

'Arrest this man, Sheriff!' he ordered, ignoring the six-shooter held on them belly-high. 'Dillard, you're fired!'

'I've quit anyhow.'

There was no telling how the tense situation would have resolved itself without the intervention of Sophie Vickers.

She was a woman with a mind of her own and staying outside, standing meekly with the sweating steeldust, its head hanging after carrying its double load to the cabin, didn't fit one jot with her plans. She marched into the cabin, past the arguing men, and slapped the face of the hapless Liberty Tolliver where she cowered on the rope bed, hemmed up in a corner.

'You're a tramp, Liberty Tolliver!'

Liberty, shocked and open-mouthed, took the blow that reddened her pale cheek with the merest whimper, as though she was insensible to any further indignity that could be inflicted on her.

'Hey! Cut that out!' Joshua said. 'Didn't I tell you to stay outside?'

A fight between the two women in the crowded cabin could easily descend into a fracas in which the control he'd imposed at gunpoint would be nullified by the likelihood of the unintentional deaths of the wrong people. Vickers and Lant might deserve anything chance dealt them, but Joshua had no desire to face a murder charge for shooting a woman or women.

'If you don't intend to put a slug in my bastard of a husband, give me my pistol back!' Sophie cried.

'Haven't you a lick of sense, Mrs Vickers?' Joshua said. 'Get right outa the way, you hear me! Go back outside!'

But Sophie was intent on creating disturbance.

'Don't you tell me what to do! And you, Barnaby Lant, what do you think you're doing here? Interfering with and sharing ranch-trollop trash! What would our father have said?'

Vickers sniggered. 'Stubborn as hell, that wife of mine. Bossy, like old Adam Lant was.'

Joshua said, 'I'm not interested in

your family feuding, any of you. Lant, you're getting out. Mrs Tolliver, you'd best get yourself covered and come with me. Vickers, you and your damnfool wife can have your fight if you like, but I'm taking all the guns.'

Vickers grinned, this time malevolently.

'Nope. I think not, Mr Wise-Guy. You've bitten off more than you can chew. Now if you'd like to drop your gun and turn around, you'll see what I mean. Never keep your back to a door — comeuppance is liable to creep up right behind you!'

Joshua laughed at him. 'Only a greenhorn in the lawdog business would fall for that one, Vickers.'

That was when the back of his head was violently struck.

A chaos of impressions followed. The faces of Vickers, Lant and the two women took flight and soared upwards, as though they were leaving the floor. But then it was the floor itself that was coming up to meet his face in a rush of disorientation. He was tumbling; the whole world was dissolving into roaring, blinding blackness.

Sound and sight hightailed it into the distance. Oblivion took over. He never heard or felt the smack when he hit the floor.

7

Missing Guns

Joshua was smack-dab in the middle of a dream in which he was drowning in a river in rushing flood when he was jolted back rudely to consciousness. He spluttered and spat.

More water hit his face thrown from a bucket over which loomed a face he knew and didn't expect to see.

'That'll do, Mr McGill!' he said, lifting a stalling hand and raising himself on his other elbow. He was still on the floor in Vickers' cabin. His memory was sound, but he'd been dispossessed of his revolver and Sophie Vickers' hideout gun was no longer in his pocket.

'What happened here?' he asked.

Crazy Bob's whiskery face creased up in frowning puzzlement.

'Can't rightly tell. You're the stranger that helped me out last night. Didn't expect to see you here. And Missus Vickers, she's been trussed up tight as a fowl for roasting.'

Rising from the floor, Joshua saw for himself that Sophie was not only efficiently bound to a heavy pine chair but gagged. Evidently more than one person hadn't wanted to listen to her shrill accusations. She'd been acting like a woman fit to be tied before his hand in the game — whatever the game was — had been trumped.

Dan Vickers and Barnaby Lant were gone, of course. So was Liberty Tolliver. From what he'd witnessed, the young woman hadn't been at the cabin willingly. Joshua didn't think she would have gone with the men willingly either, and he found her absence disturbing.

'I figure you've some talking to do, old-timer. It was your note that sent Mrs Vickers here like a bat out of hell, wasn't it? How did you think that would help your daughter?'

The old man wilted under Joshua's accusing glare.

'What her husband was doing was wrong. I wanted to stop it. I thought maybe *she* would do it.'

Joshua shook his head wearily. 'A mistake.'

'I know. But I was real mad about it. I rode out here to see the outcome — to see if Sophie had fixed the business.'

'No. She got fixed herself, it looks. So did I. You'd've done better if you'd gotten your girl a good lawyer. It didn't look to me like she wanted to be here. She was acting under duress, I reckon. Vickers should be charged and held to account in a court. Hell, if they knew how it was, any jury on earth would find Vickers guilty.'

McGill rejected Joshua's suggestion vehemently.

'I'd not want my daughter drug up before no man jury! She'd have to tell ever'thing that happened. You know how the shysters are on that kinda case.

They don't let a woman alone till she spills all the details of whatever hold the louse has gotten over her; how he used her. Her name would be ruined — she'd be like a girl who was Indian-took and forced to serve the bucks. No man or woman would give her any respect.'

Joshua knew about it. Sadly, it was the way a generation thought. Nothing one man could do would bring about change. Abused and deserted Anglo-Saxon women were fallen women. Unless they had the wherewithal to start a new life someplace else, they joined the non-white — the half-breed, the Indian and the Chinese — in the bordellos. Sinned-against women were regarded as creatures of low morals, expected to maintain their broken lives by offering their spoiled bodies for money and trinkets.

He sighed heavily.

'I'd like to think your daughter has a better future. Let's free Mrs Vickers and see if she can tell us what happened to her and me.'

In the matter of Liberty Tolliver, Sophie was without sympathy. The gag taken from her mouth, she let forth a stream of invective from which Liberty wasn't excluded.

Joshua and Crazy Bob could only let the she-blister scream herself out. Then Joshua asked, 'Who knocked me cold?'

'Daniel's deputy — the one they call Gus Kurtz,' she said tartly. 'He sneaked in behind you. And you were too smart to believe my rat of a husband when he told you!'

Joshua nodded, suppressing his irritation as he remembered the beefy fellow who'd swapped blows with him at the sheriff's office. 'That figures. This Kurtz acts like he was your spouse's guard dog. To boot, he's considerable fond of laying gun barrels across heads.'

He wondered what it was that made the sheriff's deputy so desperate to cover his boss's tail. Deputies were seldom so loyal, and a fall from grace by a superior was frequently the forerunner to their own advancement in the electoral stakes.

Joshua touched his scalp, finding a blood-sticky gash he estimated was two inches long. For a fit person, serious problems were rare from a mild head injury. His vision was fine. He knew where he was and wasn't the least confused, other than by his difficult companions and the situation he'd come across in the Redstone cow-country. Grumpy or irritable? Yeah — likewise with the said companions.

He wasn't vomiting or shaking either. Sure, he had a headache and felt tired, but he wasn't badly concussed. His mind was clear about what he should do.

He had to get astride the steeldust and follow Lant and Vickers. Rescuing Liberty Tolliver from their clutches was the very least he could do to salvage something — self-respect maybe — from a sorry episode in his trouble-busting career.

McGill had about given up his daughter for lost; Sophie Vickers didn't give a damn for anything except her wounded pride and exacting revenge out of all proportion.

He looked around and saw no trace of his Peacemaker. He rechecked his pockets. Nor did he have Sophie's derringer any longer.

Sophie laughed mockingly. 'They've drawn your fighting teeth, big man.' She picked up and opened her reticule, showing it was innocent of weaponry; she spread her arms. 'I don't have my pistol back either. You can check if you like.'

Joshua wasn't going to pat her down. The smoothly voluptuous bumps and curves she had under her green silk dress were uninterrupted by the stubby contours of a five-inch-plus hunk of nickel-plated, pearl-gripped gun metal.

'That won't be necessary,' Joshua said in an acid tone. 'Did they say where they were going?'

'My pathetic brother and my randy husband?'

'Who else? Them and Gus Kurtz.

Where did they take Mrs Tolliver?'

Sophie's amusement became vicious. 'They took the harlot to the Flying L.'

'Why would the sheriff go there?'

She lifted her shoulders and twisted her mouth as though disinterested.

'My brother had complaints. The lawdogs need to do some sniffing. And I'm sure they'll enjoy Mrs Tolliver's modest, wifely charms.'

Joshua winced, McGill moaned despairingly, and Sophie plunged on, enjoying what she had to report.

'They said that when the bitch was used up, she could be thrown into service in the bunkhouse for a few nights, to pay for her keep.'

Gun or no gun, getting to the Flying L was now the first object in Joshua's mind. Yet it was a goal set to be denied. On going to the door of the cabin, he found the steeldust nowhere in sight. His horse, though a docile, tractable critter and just about played out, had been stripped and taken or run off.

His saddle and bedroll, the damp

Navajo horse blanket and ransacked bags, had been dumped in a heap in the dust out front.

Joshua swore. What now?

He studied on his options. Nothing was just going to happen; resolutions had to be brought about. His thinking produced an imperfect course of action, but one that would have to answer several problems simultaneously.

He turned to McGill, hoping he could trust the old man who'd given up on his violated daughter to do something right.

'I'll stay here and keep an eye on Mrs Vickers. I want you to ride your horse back to town. Borrow or rent a buckboard, buggy or similar and bring it back here. Also hire a fresh saddle mount and tie it on behind. And bring me a serviceable handgun, preferably a Colt, with ammunition . . . Here, I still have enough greenbacks left to cover most of it.'

Crazy Bob scratched his head.

'So what'll be your plan?'

'This. You'll return Mrs Vickers to the safety of her home and haberdashery, using the borrowed rig. I'll ride to the Flying L on the fresh mount and do what I can for Mrs Tolliver — and to clean out a nest of snakes. I've a hunch more's afoot than has been let on. Since I figure to get to the bottom of it, there'll be scant use in going off half-cocked.'

Naturally enough, Sophie Vickers had something to say.

'You're a fool, Mr Dillard. You should accept that Barnaby doesn't want you after all and quit while you've got a whole skin. You'll never get to know the half of it.'

Joshua didn't try to make anything of Sophie's cryptic statement. He'd had a bellyful of the dressed-to-kill woman and her tinbadge husband, a fancy-pants puppet plainly installed in office by her family's money.

He let her have the truth of it.

'Too bad my plans don't fit in with your'n. If you think I'm going to light a shuck and you'll straighten out your marital affairs with another pistol, you're plain wrong.'

She snorted with disgust, but avoided looking him in the eye.

'We'll see, Mr Dillard. We'll see.'

* * *

More than two hours elapsed before Crazy Bob McGill returned with Joshua's requests carried out. Joshua had calculated this would be the case and had been prepared for an uncomfortable interlude at the cabin with Sophie Vickers. Handsome woman though she was, she bristled most of the time like a cat with an intruder on its territory.

They avoided conversing and without means of transport neither was prepared to stray far along the lake's shore from the cabin. The best that could be said was that the scenery was stunning and the weather beautiful. By and large, Joshua expected this in Montana. The summer tended to be dry. Sunshine was the norm; only a few days produced cloud and light rain. Yet, despite the abundant sun, the temperature wasn't too hot at the lake's elevation and the pine stands cast long, cool shadows.

Too bad little was right in this paradise.

* * *

Range detective! Sophie Vickers saw plenty to despise in Joshua Dillard's secondhand range garb. He looked like a dumb-stupid saddle bum. He'd surely be proved exactly that when he tangled with her two-timing sheriff husband and the might of the Lant family — albeit her brother was not the man their father had been.

She'd let them take care of Dillard, as they inevitably would, then she'd make her own play and claim her own retribution.

For she knew where her derringer was. It wasn't with Dan, Barnaby or

Gus Kurtz. They'd confiscated Dillard's guns all right, but the small pistol had slipped from the pocket of her star-toting spouse's gray California pants, fashionably patched and foxed with buckskin and tucked into highly polished boots.

Both she and Liberty Tolliver had given the three men trouble: a mêlée had ensued after Dillard had been knocked out cold and before she could be ignominiously tied to a chair. Liberty had bitten Dan. The small thud the tiny pistol had made when it dropped to the floor had gone unnoticed; likewise, the sharp kick Sophie had delivered the gun, sending it spinning behind a Shoshone-woven willow basket containing firewood.

When the time was ripe, she meant to reclaim her hidden property from beside the lava-rock fireplace and resume her mission.

Patience was not Sophie's strong suit. But she spent the tedious two hours Crazy Bob McGill was gone gloating in her imagination over the shootings of Daniel Vickers and Liberty Tolliver.

The adulterers might be safe from her wrath for the moment, but the Flying L headquarters would not provide them sanctuary for long.

8

Cottonwood Justice

Joshua Dillard was in sight of Lant's substantial ranch house. Prosperous-looking, it sprawled long, low and rambling on a bench across a valley, overlooking an assortment of barns, other sturdily constructed outbuildings and pole corrals. In another place and time, its dominance would have been that of a manor house surrounded by its village.

He reined up the leggy sorrel mare McGill had brought him from town, and pulled a pair of field glasses from his saddlebag.

He reflected, sardonically, that although Barnaby Lant, Dan Vickers and Gus Kurtz might be good at taking what wasn't legally theirs, they weren't petty thieves. They hadn't stolen the glasses,

119

which were German-made and good.

Joshua focused the glasses across-valley and swept the facing slopes. His attention was caught immediately by a bustle of activity near a bosque of cottonwoods. He recognized some of the riders as men he'd seen at the Flying L's round-up camp — the surly hand he suspected was gunfighter Tex Pynchon and gruff ramrod Carl Pederson were among them.

They were escorting a man lying over his bronc's saddle, his wrists anchored to one cinch ring, his cowboy-booted ankles to the other. Was he dead . . . or just a hog-tied prisoner?

Joshua muttered an oath. There was something plumb funny going on here — in point of fact, the whole set-up in this Redstone Gulch section smacked of funny business. It was one of the locoest situations he'd ever run up against.

The top dog, Barnaby Lant, had lost or was losing his grip, hiring outlaw trash to hold onto his range, most of which probably was Uncle Sam's.

The local law which was supposedly in Lant's pocket seemed anywhere but . . . like, in the drawers of a woman selling her soul. Not an entirely new trick for Sheriff Dan Vickers, since Redstone scuttlebutt suggested he couldn't leave pretty women alone and 'fishing' at Devil's Lake was a bluff he'd run before.

Meanwhile, Lant's freshly enlightened sister — no cattle queen but the lawman's cheated wife — was a menace to everyone, doing a headstrong impersonation of Nemesis, goddess of revenge.

Now there was a bunch of Flying L men with a mystery captive that went from the field glasses' view, lost among the cottonwoods.

Joshua was about to put the glasses away when more movement from the direction of the Lant ranch house caught his attention. He raised the glasses again.

Two riders had headed out from the house and gave the impression they were making tracks for the same clump of cottonwoods. An overhanging, faint smudge of gray dust marked their progress.

The rider leading the way was Jim Stebbings, the friendly young puncher who'd filled him in on the lie of the land when he'd met him at the round-up camp.

The second man was Barnaby Lant on a big claybank, his bulk hunched in the saddle, falling behind a mite and eating his hand's dust. Even through glasses, Joshua could pick up from his posture and what looked like a grimace on a bleak face that he was in a dark mood.

The pair completed their descent from the bench and continued their ride toward the cottonwoods through tall bluejoint grass and sagebrush. The soil of the bottomlands was fertile, kept moist year-round by rain and the runoff from the surrounding mountains. It supported fine pasture growth. Joshua judged Lant's little empire to be excellent cattle country of the kind that had originally lured men from the South to 'Montany'.

Lost from sight from time to time, the passage of Stebbings and Lant was marked by plump sage hens that flew from under their feet in stately flight on mottled, yellow-brown wings.

Joshua considered his options. He could proceed on a straight course to the Lant ranch headquarters, where he assumed he'd find Liberty Tolliver and Dan Vickers, or he could ride down into the valley and snoop on what was playing out under the cottonwoods.

It was no easy choice, but he decided in favor of the latter. He neck-reined the sorrel mare around and pointed her down-slope.

Nearing the bosque, he headed into a brush-grown draw to hide his approach from the roughneck Flying L crew as long as possible. He figured they wouldn't welcome his showing-up at all. And if Barnaby Lant was on the scene before him, a hot reception was guaranteed.

Joshua reached the fringe of the cottonwoods and jumped down from his horse. He didn't trust her to stand on trailing reins, but hitched her to a sturdy sapling. Then he crept forward, staying concealed from the men whose voices were now being raised stridently in the hidden depths of the wood.

Pederson was putting what sounded like a case to Barnaby Lant.

'The boys say hang the bastard, Mr Barnaby. Ain't no skin offa our noses what they does, I say. They ain't had much o' their sorta fun since they hired on for us. They're feelin' awful mean an' frisky . . . Let 'em do it!'

Tex Pynchon chimed in.

'He was caught wideloopin' your fat li'le brutes, boss. Redhanded! An' stringin' up's the penalty fer rustlin' another man's stock where I come from.'

Joshua peered round a wide bole.

He saw Barnaby Lant scratching his massive head.

'Well, I don't know it'd be lawful, and Tolliver here — he couldn't be organizing the running-off of whole herds. Ain't got the brains for it. I reckon he reasoned just no one would know what he was doing — seeing even his wife wasn't at home. To boot, he'd conveniently arranged for our friend Sheriff Vickers to be absent from his duties fulfilling a long-time ambition to entertain the said wife.'

'Yeah, your *friend* the sheriff, boss!' Pynchon crowed. 'We can hang this rustler an' not have nothin' to mind law-badge-wise!'

Tom Tolliver, unleashed from his horse, was in shirtsleeves and levis. Hatless and white-faced, he was a middle-aged man, suddenly showing all his years. Fate had dealt him a second, ironic swipe. Seeking to take what advantage he could of its first swipe — discovery of his original rustling crimes by Sheriff Dan Vickers and the payoff the lawman had demanded — he'd been run across by several of the Flying

125

L outfit returning from their cow camp.

When he spoke, Tolliver's voice trembled through fear.

'I didn't do it!' he said unconvincingly. 'There ain't no evidence!'

'There are so, Tolliver,' Pederson said. 'We saw a calf sportin' your Rockin' T that ran to its Flyin' L mama and started suckin'.'

Pynchon laughed cynically. 'Yeah, we all saw that — it was plain an' obvious. The calf's brand was half-fresh. Still smokin', yuh c'd say!'

Tolliver's eyes met nothing but gazes of accusation.

'Then — then, it wasn't me!' he blurted.

Pynchon, eager to be done with parleying, was scathing.

'Aw, pull the other leg, lunkhead! Yuh was found not a mile off, packin' the runnin' iron yuh done it with — an' ropin' another Flyin' L calf!'

'I — I thought it was a maverick!' Tolliver said, his lies getting frantic.

A calf that was still a cow's suckling

should bear the adult critter's brand, or no brand. That stood to reason and was an unwritten law all over the West

It hit Joshua how easily a Flying L brand could be altered so it would read as a Rocking T. The upright of the L had a wing-like wiggle at the top, to its left, that suggested the letter was 'flying'. The device could be extended to the right in a straight line to make it the top bar of a T. Then the baseline of the L could be similarly lengthened, but with a more curving sweep to the left of the upright. After a little aging, the result would pass muster as conforming with the conventions used to denote a 'rocking' letter T.

Joshua's contempt for this Tom Tolliver grew. The same man who could evidently abandon a pretty young wife to a Lothario also showed himself to be an idiot if he expected crude theft, once detected, to go unpunished. Joshua wondered if Tolliver had been caught at such low-scale rustling before. Was that the explanation of the hold Vickers had over Liberty Tolliver?

'Time's a-wastin', Mr Barnaby,' Pederson growled. 'Let an example be made of Tolliver. You got nothin' to lose.'

'But is it all legal . . . ?'

'Who's to say — 'cept Dirty Dan Vickers? He's your Redstone bailiwick's law. Mebbe the real rustlers'll think twice if'n they think you're a harder man than your departed pa.'

Lant frowned. 'You likely had help, Tolliver. Some of them riff-raff folk outa the hills, maybe. Who was your flanking-man?'

Pederson snarled, 'He's too dumb to talk and save his skin. Get this over with!'

Tolliver squealed and, though his wrists were still tied, he tried to make a break for freedom. A roughneck stuck a boot in his path, pushed, and his shambling run ended in a gale of mocking laughter.

'All right,' Lant said morosely. 'Tolliver, you're a loser who never learns. My crew's blood is up. It's agreed you should be hanged.'

Notably, only Jim Stebbings looked sickened by Lant's decision. His face was white as a death-mask. In bringing the cattle baron here, maybe he'd hoped for a better outcome.

'Is this the right way to take care of a stupid no-account? The right way of justice?'

'You shut your mouth, kid!' Pederson ordered. 'It's a chore gotta be done an' we don't have to dirty our hands. Consider it a matter of honor, see? That's a powerful thing. If'n Tolliver gets away with the rebrandin', Mr Lant and the Flyin' L'll lose face and look weak in the eyes of the whole range. Other small fry'll foller Tolliver's example — take what they like, how they like.'

The hardcases whooped. A rope was flung up over a horizontal cottonwood limb at a convenient height. Tolliver was manhandled to his horse and into the saddle. A dark patch appeared on his left pants leg. He'd wet himself, which occasioned more vulgar mirth among the sweaty hands.

Joshua reached for the Colt brought him by Crazy Bob McGill, yet changed his mind the minute his fingers touched the butt. He shrugged inwardly.

It was damnable, but he could do nothing to save Tom Tolliver. He was hopelessly outnumbered here. Moreover, Tolliver was despicable and he was wasting what might be his best chance to rescue the cowardly rancher's unfortunate wife.

It was time to pull up stakes unless he wanted to lose the advantage the general preoccupation within the gloom of the bosque might give him at Lant's headquarters yonder.

He'd seen men hanged before; seen others, men and women both, stare on in wide-eyed horror and fascination. That wasn't for him. He slipped away from the tawdry perversion of justice being acted out in the somber shadows of the cottonwoods. He went as silently as he had come.

He regained the sorrel's saddle and put Tolliver's yells and sobs behind him, faded rapidly by distance. But his skin crawled.

9

Something to Remember

Joshua Dillard concentrated his thoughts on his original intention. That had been to ride to the Flying L, to brace and have a reckoning with the men who'd knocked him cold, stolen his gun, likely run off the steeldust . . . left him unconscious up at an isolated lake with a tied and gagged woman for company.

And, it might be added, one very mad woman.

From Sophie Vickers, his thoughts went to the second woman in the case.

He also intended to free his offenders' other prisoner, the daughter of Crazy Bob McGill, Mrs Liberty Tolliver. Now her husband was hanged, the attraction in that was lessened. For when he saved her he would also have to tell her she was a widow — though, he had to ask himself, would that be any great blow?

These plans were ambitious enough for any one man. Once they were accomplished, Joshua would be glad to call his latest, unrewarding mission to Montana finished. He wouldn't want to linger. The section should have been a cowman's paradise, but it was under the shadow of a coming range war. Having met some of the likely combatants, he saw no clear part in it for himself.

With his erstwhile client, Barnaby Lant, absent from the Flying L headquarters, Joshua anticipated opposition to his plans would come primarily from Sheriff Dan Vickers and his deputy, Gus Kurtz.

Lant and his law-badge-toting tool had plainly assumed his 'I quit' had signaled he was giving up on the case altogether and immediately; that he would, on coming to his senses, lick his wounds, free Mrs Vickers and leave the Redstone country as best and as soon as he could.

They didn't know Joshua, or that since his wife's murder by ruthless criminals he'd devoted long years to righting cruelty and injustice, especially to powerless women.

He figured his chances were good of catching Vickers and Kurtz unawares at the Flying L. The outfit's more dangerous elements — its hardcase crew of hired guns and the unpredictable Lant himself — were down among the cottonwoods behind him, attending to the lynching of Tom Tolliver.

It had already been one hell of a long and rough day. As he rode over the lush green grassland, Joshua's blood quickened at the prospect of a swift resolution.

Unfortunately, it turned out to be yet another of those occasions when the recklessness which had effectively terminated his usefulness to the Pinkerton agency proved the undoing of his scheme.

* * *

Liberty Tolliver had greeted her removal from the lakeside cabin to the Flying L ranch house with a degree of relief, despite the threats her persecutors made. At a busy, working ranch, surely Vickers and Lant would have less opportunity and time for pestering her.

Lant was riled by the latest tally on his stock. It showed a considerable depletion of which the only explanation could be wholesale rustling. He was demanding Vickers put his work — namely, investigating as sheriff of the county — before his play — namely, her.

But Liberty's relief proved short-lived.

She was hustled into a big front parlor. The Flying L ranch-house was a pretentious creation. Adam Lant had allowed it to expand like his spread. It was long, low and rambling, flaunting the Flying L's wealth. Old Adam had spared no expense to make the place one he considered worthy of his family's residency.

Although it was summer, embers glowed in the big stone fireplace and the odor of burning pine mingled with the smell of the leather of well-stuffed armchairs and couches. Liberty's nose detected also overlying whiffs of liquor, tobacco and sweaty horseflesh. Big windows were thrown wide onto a front gallery.

But Liberty had barely had time to note the luxury of the Flying L compared to her own humble home on Tom Tolliver's Rocking T when an excited young hand rode pell-mell into the yard. She knew him of old from his attendance at bygone town dances. He pulled his horse to a slithering halt. Rocks were gouged out, crunched and scattered from under the iron-shod hoofs. Dust rose in billows. The hand jumped down.

'Mr Lant! Mr Lant, sir!'

Barnaby Lant went out onto the gallery, scowling. 'What the hell is it, Stebbings?'

The words came from Stebbings in

one long, breathless tumble.

'The cow-camp crew caught Tom Tolliver at work with a runnin' iron . . . on Flyin' L calves. They're organizin' a neck-tie party, down among the cotton-woods. Less'n you come fast, he's gonna dance on air!'

Lant turned to Vickers and Kurtz.

'I better go,' he said reluctantly. 'Take care of that damn woman, Vickers! It's about all you're fit for. You should've figured Tolliver might try more of his fool games, specially knowing he'd gotten you occupied at the lake.'

He stomped off, calling for a fresh horse.

Liberty's heart was in her mouth. Her stupid husband had run his neck into a noose. Damn him! It sounded like he'd fallen into the hands of a lynch mob.

It was a measure of her disgrace that no one queried her lack of visible, emotional response to the trouble her husband was in. She did indeed feel strangely empty once past the moment of stunned horror. She wanted only to forget him.

Nor was Vickers in any wise discomposed by Lant's censure of his shortcomings in upholding the law on the range. He gritted *sotto voce* as Lant went out of hearing, 'It'd give me pleasure to take care of Mrs Tolliver, Barnaby ol' pal. She fires the blood more'n your cold sister ever did!'

Kurtz said, 'Didn't one of us oughta go along with Lant, Dan?'

Vickers shook his head. 'No way. The law won't even know about a hanging, savvy? That way our noses are kept clean.'

'Why, yeah . . . I see what you mean.'

'Tolliver will have to take care of his own troubles; take whatever comes.'

Kurtz smiled. 'Sure. We gotta keep playing the game smart. Senseless to horn in to get someone else outa a hole.'

'You got it. Now while I'm attending to Mrs Tolliver's — uh — comfort, why don't you jus' have a mosey along and check that all's well around Mr Lant's fine home place?'

Liberty shuddered when Vickers caught hold of her hand and swung her away from the windows across the room.

'Looks like you're gonna miss out on kissing goodbye to your skunk of a husband, Mrs Tolliver. Though way I figure it, he's kinda sold your kisses anyways.'

Without further ado, he pushed her down on a couch and threw himself on top of her.

She was past struggle; past unheeded protest. She felt no marital obligation to Tolliver and had already been subjected to a night of bestial attack with his connivance.

Vickers yanked open her cotton blouse and the four front buttons of the white, cording-reinforced corset beneath, exposing again the roundness of her breasts.

'This is crazy,' she said. 'Lant's thugs are trying to hang my husband. Shouldn't you be doing something?'

'T' hell with Tolliver! Your man's sad comeuppance ain't no never-mind, gal.' Vickers chuckled lasciviously. 'What's more, I am doing something, ain't I?'

It wasn't easy for Liberty to admit that the man she'd agreed to marry wasn't really a man at all; that he was some kind of idiot and a rat. Always grossly effusive with his sham good nature and heartiness, he was at bottom a weak and cowardly man who'd exploited and degraded her to save his own skin.

Head swimming, she arrived at the bleak conclusion that her sacrifice to appease Vickers had been all for nothing. The truth was that right now she was in just as harrowing a tight as she was going to be if Tolliver did dance to a deserved death at the end of a hangrope.

What if Dan Vickers made her pregnant? What if she were to become a mother as well as a widow?

'Please,' she said. 'Get off me. Leave me alone. Go after the others.'

'No, damn you! Stop twisting and squirming and turning your head!'

'I can't do what you want. I'm not a whore.'

He was cynically amused.

'That's a poor lie in light of recent showing,' he scoffed. 'Most every wife hankers to be a whore when marital bedding palls. Spread your knees; work!'

Liberty gave in. She'd humored him a whole grueling night before. It would be absurd, and better her plight not one iota, to act the prim ingénue. This had no reality, no direct meaning to her. It was only sex after all, nothing more. No part of her. No part of her life. Again, she surrendered to the punishment of his attentions.

She wished to God it was over with. She strived for and achieved a measure of mental detachment, but it was impossible not to gasp and groan aloud in response to ruthless use. Minutes passed uncounted, dragging in the tracks of her annihilated honor.

* ★ ★

The Flying L ranch looked as deserted at closer quarters as it had from a distance. But Joshua Dillard knew he was stepping onto dangerous ground by walking into the Lant stronghold.

Barnaby Lant, though apparently under siege from enemies seeking to make good old losses after his powerful father's demise, had hired a pack of gun wolves. And he still had the local sheriff in his pocket, too.

Vickers might no longer be of any large account, since he chose to be ineffective in exercising his authority, bought or otherwise. But with scant pretense of a rule of law, assaults, lynchings and shootings would go unchecked in the Redstone country. Joshua's elimination would pass unnoticed amidst the mayhem of a range war.

Joshua had the nagging doubt at the back of his mind that Sophie Vickers' assessment had been right — he was embarked on foolishness and time-wasting. But the unresolved mysteries and the plight of a young, abused wife were playing havoc with his peace of mind for reasons buried deep in his own history and the code by which he lived his odd life.

He scooted from building to building, hugging the afternoon's shadows. He passed a cook shack window on noiseless feet. Inside he saw one small sign of activity on the property. A Chinese ranch cook, flour sack tied around his midriff, peeled potatoes. His fingers were nimble and swift. His concentration on the chore looked absolute.

Joshua gained the gallery that fronted the imposing ranch house. Through windows flung wide came the sound of a woman's frantic appeals.

'No! No! Not again . . . ah, my God! Have mercy on me!'

Disgusted by what he knew he was about to witness, Joshua stepped into the big front parlor through the open doors.

'That'll be all, Vickers!' he said. 'This time you're on your own, and it won't take a gun to teach you a lesson in conduct with womenfolk.'

'The sticky beak!' Vickers cried. 'Whadya think you're doing here, Dillard?'

'I'm here to smash the daylights out of your miserable carcass. After that, I'll see Mrs Tolliver home.'

'Like hell you will!'

Vickers got to his feet, buttoning his pants.

'He raped me,' Liberty sobbed unnecessarily, pulling the strategic portions of her disarranged clothing back into place.

Vickers ignored her and the charge; she might not have spoken. He stood his ground, regarding Joshua with an arrogant, pale-eyed, unblinking stare. From habit, he was confident in the superiority bestowed upon him by a metal star.

'You've no authority to be here, Dillard,' he said. 'You were lucky to be left alive at the lake. Now you're trespassing again on private property, interfering in business that's none of your'n. My orders for you are to quit Redstone County before you get hurt plenty bad.'

Joshua saw red. He had nothing but contempt for this Fancy, Dirty Dan who pinned to his stylish clothes a badge to which he added no luster.

'Bastard!' he growled. 'You'll let Mrs Tolliver leave with me. Stand aside, before I knock you clear across the parlor!'

Vickers, snarled, 'She was willing. She's going no place.'

'Says you!'

Joshua's right arm swung, hand clenched to form a rock-hard fist. He caught the smirking dude with a crisp smack on the point of his jaw. It sent him stumbling back on the heels of his polished boots.

Vickers swore and, balance regained, he lunged back, his own fists balled.

Shocked, Liberty said, 'He's the

sheriff of the county, Mr Dillard . . . do like he says and ride out while you can!'

Joshua's answer was to duck Vickers' wild blows and bore in, arms working like pistons, delivering a series of short, pummeling punches to his chest and solar plexus.

'No,' he grunted almost to himself. 'I'm going to give this low-down cur something to remember.'

Vickers was driven back again, winded. As law boss of Redstone, backed by the Lant fortune, he'd grown complacent and soft in body. Joshua's fists sank deep into the flesh of sybaritic living.

Joshua figured the odds were in his favor. A life of bitterness, hardship and constant activity had made him whip-cord and steel. Before Vickers could regain his breath and put up his guard, he aimed to mark up his handsome face. He'd leave him carrying scars more evident than his victim's to remind him indulgence of lust came at a price.

He smashed two blows at Vickers' face. They bruised flesh and brought blood that trickled from his swollen nose into his mouth.

But Vickers came back, driven by his rage at the upstart range detective hired and fired by Barnaby Lant. Joshua didn't know where the dude found the strength for it. He made a grab for Joshua's arm; caught a hold and twisted.

Joshua used his knee and pulled free. His fists beat a quick tattoo that bloodied Vickers' face some more and further slackened the progress of the fight.

They circled, making wary jabs with their fists till Vickers bumped into a table and half-fell over one of its chairs. It was a heavy, gothic piece with square back and seat, both well padded, and turned front legs. With the strength of desperation, Vickers seized it by the back, straightened up, and swung it high.

Joshua saw it coming back down

toward his head at express-train speed and knew fists and arms would be useless at warding off the skull-shattering blow.

10

Cowpuncher's Choice

The little Chinese ranch cook paid no attention to the occasional, female cries that emanated from the boss's big house. It was not for the lowly Wong-See to understand the strange customs of the white race.

In his Oriental world, women did not utter cries, be they of protest or pleasure or pain. Decorum permitted only sighs, never shrieks. Women were kept, in all respects, subjugated. They were never alone with casual male acquaintances.

Here, it seemed, the treatment of women was altogether different. And he knew girls of his own race were frequently kidnapped by, or sold for pennies to, the American slave traders. In the big city of San Francisco the best were auctioned to the bidders of hundreds of dollars to be put to work as prostitutes in brothels or cribs.

It was dollars that had brought Wong-See himself to this Frontier West from the Middle Kingdom in pursuit of a dream: to make enough money to return to China with his savings for a life of ease, surrounded and honored by a family whom his foreign toils would sustain.

He steadfastly peeled potatoes, his face the acceptable, expressionless mask of inscrutability.

But the sounds of wholly male rage, of fighting and damage to his master's property, brought his detachment to an abrupt end. He put down his peeling knife and left the cook shack to investigate. He sped cautiously on felt-slippered feet — the loose sleeves of his jacket flapping, his pigtail swinging — to a place alongside the hands' empty bunkhouse that gave him an unimpeded view of the front of the ranch house.

Through the big parlor windows he saw glimpses of a vicious fist-fight in progress between two men. He recognized one of the men as Sheriff Dan Vickers, who was the friend of his master. The other was a stranger.

Were they fighting over the woman?

Had not Wong-See better get help for Vickers?

The sheriff's assistant, the one they called Deputy Kurtz, was on the ranch, probably close by, since he had not seen him leave when the master had left urgently, presumably to join his crew after the young hand called Jim Stebbings had arrived to fetch him.

The conflict unfolding within the survey of the Chinese cook's narrow, black eyes was afforded his impassive consideration.

Very soon, he nodded his head to himself. It would pay him to seek help. He went in search of Kurtz, whom he'd last seen moseying alone in the direction of the horse corral.

★ ★ ★

Jim Stebbings had known for months that the brand he rode for was heading down the trail to perdition. Strained though it had been by Barnaby Lant's hiring of gunfighter trash, only a very stubborn loyalty had kept him from rolling his blankets and heading out from the Flying L.

Maybe the whole of Montana was fast going to hell as far as peaceable cattle country was concerned. He had his theories about that, and about the rustling that was depleting the Flying L herds.

He also believed he had a notion who was behind the organization of the wholesale rustling. It was sound but startling, and the worst of it was he had no evidence to back it, or the status or means to put the matter to rights. Sure as shooting, Barnaby Lant was being bamboozled and Tom Tolliver's involvement in the main game, if any, had been small beer.

Likewise, although they might be rogues to a man and bore watching, the trash who ranched in the badlands of the foothills, living in hovels with slatternly wives and hordes of brats, weren't the real villains.

Jim had been sickened by the hanging of Tom Tolliver.

The grisly business completed, Barnaby Lant, sensing his hard-bitten crew expected further reward, cleared his throat with a rattling sound intended to sound authoritative. He made the announcement that the hanged man's wife was at the Flying L headquarters under the 'protection' of Sheriff Dan Vickers — known to even the newest of the imported Flying L gunhawks as Dirty Dan.

'The woman's asked for it. You'll get to have a free hand there, I guess. Our tame tinbadge don't look for lasting commitments and his blessing's a fair bet . . . '

The word gave rise to excited conjecture among the rough outfit, as Lant must have calculated it would.

Ribald suggestions passed from man to man that the co-operative sheriff might be prevailed upon to allow the bunch to assist him in the comfort of the new widow.

'The dude wouldn't want to keep the chore to hisself, would he now?'

'No skin offa his nose to share it around. They do say he changes women as often as other men change their socks.'

There was a deal of similar innuendo and winking and guffawing.

'The poor li'le wife didn't git no fond farewell from her departed Tolliver.'

'Aw, now ain't that a shame? Someone'll have to do it for the bastard, Tex.'

'Say, can I volunteer?'

Pynchon spat out the butt of a dead quirly from between his stained teeth.

'Damnit, Lew, we'll all take turns! I think I seen Tolliver's woman an' she's got plenty to go round afore she'll look used up.'

The mood was infectious and had the

effect Lant desired.

'What about it, Mr Lant?' he was asked.

He shrugged. 'Anything you do with Mrs Tolliver meets with my complete approval.'

His mongrel toughs entertained pleasurable thoughts and relaxed.

And this suited Jim. He allowed his horse to slip well behind the grinning bunch that spurred its way back toward the home lot in expectation of more nauseating sport.

Eventually, with a grassy ridge between himself and the body of the riders, he reined up, swung his horse's head and cantered off in a different direction from his Flying L fellows, few of whom he would consider partners. Workaday cowhands were scarce on the present Lant payroll.

Not turning back to check whether his defection was noticed — he was sure it wasn't — he set a course for the foothills that were home to the small outfits who were the Flying L's enemies.

He rode fast now and was soon in dry, hardscrabble country that to his practiced eye couldn't graze one head to forty acres.

The destination he had in mind was a tawdry settlement known as Tall Trees. It was the remnants of an old logging camp used by the hill folk as a place of miserable commerce and recreation. The rickety buildings had been converted to a saloon and several small stores. The small ranchers came to Tall Trees from their depressing homes in the hills to trade in cattle, horses and other goods many claimed were stolen. Rumor also had it whiskey was peddled to Indians and the Tall Trees storekeepers were receivers of nomadic rawhiders' loot.

He urged his cow-pony to stretch its legs, asking all he could of the roan bronc. Time was of the essence to his intentions.

Jim, recognizable as a rider of the long-hated Flying L, would be regarded in Tall Trees with suspicion . . . until he could convince the riff-raff who patronized the dump that he'd left Lant's employ.

Too, he could reveal that the Flying L bully-boys had formed themselves into a lynching party and already dispensed with Tom Tolliver. Given out the right way, the grisly news would surely be met with fear and anger, for Tall Trees was close to the route used to smuggle rustled Lant beef out of the Redstone basin.

More importantly, he had few doubts it was the place where whoever masterminded the wholesale rustling recruited the men who did the cow-hazing work.

Jim Stebbings had settled on a daring scheme, but it offered the slim and only chance he thought he had of putting things to rights; of settling the hash of both the shifty-eyed Flying L crew and the slimy Sheriff Vickers.

Sadly, it was nigh on an impossibility it could be put in train quickly enough to save the unfortunate Mrs Tolliver from the fate contemplated for her by Tex Pynchon and his buddies. Jim hoped she had, and would be able to draw from, that well of strength he'd seen in the bravest of ranch women. Their day-to-day lives were frequently an ordeal. Some it left worn and haggard before they were thirty. To others, the harsh and unruly frontier lent fiber of an astonishing kind.

The wild bunch's sarcasm aside, it *was* a shame what had happened and was about to happen. Mrs Tolliver couldn't be much older than twenty-five, still a genuine beauty. And she'd always had a certain quiet dignity, a friendly and honest manner.

Jim sighed gustily. She had been way too good to have fallen into Dirty Dan's evil clutches, let alone to have married Tom Tolliver whose ethics and bonhomie had been fraudulent to his eyes way back.

He wondered briefly if, out of obedience to a misguided duty, the young woman had willingly allowed herself to become embroiled in a silly plot to divert the sheriff while her husband carried out his petty stock thieving. But he promptly dismissed the thought. She was surely too sensible, too decent.

If he could ever have afforded to court a girl on a rider's wages, Liberty McGill would — from the little he knew of her — have been exactly the kind he would have chosen.

Before her marriage, he'd partnered her a few times at the Saturday town dances in Redrock. Though he'd never hinted at his feelings in any way, there had been times when he'd felt the spirited, auburn-haired girl had understood he was an admirer and had responded in kind but unshowy ways.

But Jim had known his station in life and the meagerness of his means.

★　★　★

At the Flying L ranch house, Joshua flung himself bodily from the path of the descending chair which smashed heavily onto the floorboards in an explosion of splinters.

The heavy piece was reduced to a useless wreck. The legs and back flew off in different directions and Vickers fell forward, still clutching the padded seat.

Joshua seized the momentary advantage. As Vickers stumbled, off balance, he thrust back onto his own feet like a bouncing cat.

His hand was formed into a ruthless chopping edge that he brought down on the back of Vickers' neck at precisely the right point.

The blow brought instant senselessness to Vickers. It accelerated his stumble into a fall and deposited him in an odd, arched heap, face down on the floor, the stuffed chair seat under his midriff.

'Oh my God!' Liberty Tolliver said. 'Is he dead?'

'No, he's not, more's the pity. And it's doubtful he'll sleep for long. We've got to skedaddle, ma'am — hightail it before Lant and his killers get back.'

'Won't we be stopped?'

'I reckon not. All I've seen is a Chinese cook and I don't figure him for part of the gang. He couldn't stop us anyhow.'

Joshua paused only to recover and check his own familiar Colt Peacemaker, which he'd spied with Vickers' gunbelt discarded on a rug in front of the couch.

'Mine, I believe.'

Without asking pointless questions, as another girl might, Liberty Tolliver followed him out onto the broad front gallery.

'I've brought only one horse,' he said. 'We'll need another and there are mounts in the corrals to the left of the lot. You can sit a saddle, can't you?'

'Of course. I was raised a ranch girl,' she said, not hesitating. Then she flushed and added angrily, 'I've just been made to suffer worse than any saddle.'

Somehow, her defiant tone said he could also make what he liked of how she'd been caught in the predicament. Joshua felt keenly sorry for her in her embarrassment but couldn't find words or spare time to express any of the several layers of his sympathy.

At the end of the gallery, they ducked under its rail, jumping to the ground, and turned the corner of the house. Which was when they found themselves confronted by a major hitch.

Storming up from the corrals that were their objective came Gustav Kurtz. The Chinese cook trailed behind, wringing his hands nervously.

Kurtz had a drawn, long-barreled revolver in his right fist, and he was loaded for bear.

He saw Joshua and Liberty the moment they came into his view. His teeth bared in a snarl and he let rip an angry oath.

'Dillard! I might've guessed. And Liberty Tolliver. Where the hell do you think you're going, woman?'

'Out of here! Your Sheriff Vickers is a vile monster!'

'You better not try 'n' leave, slut. You do and it'll be the worse for Dillard and you — both!'

Joshua said, 'We go as and where we like, Deputy.'

Then Kurtz's gun swung up menacingly . . .

11

Run for Shelter

Joshua dropped to the ground, his Peacemaker slipping smoothly from its restored, holstered place on his hip into his hand.

Red flame stabbed first from Kurtz. Joshua felt the passage of his weapon's bullet as it disturbed the air a fraction of an inch above his head.

Joshua didn't like his position, nor Liberty's. They were both out in the open and it was too late to duck back into cover. Moreover, without a mount for Liberty, where could they go, where could they hide that would be beyond easy reach of the returning Flying L crew?

He had one option: to return the fire and force their way past. He triggered, blasting two shots in rapid succession.

The second was a strike that drilled Kurtz through the heart.

Kurtz had time only to give a choked sob. He was probably dead on his feet as he staggered, the six-gun slipping from his grasp to the ground with a thud. Kurtz swayed on one spot for another scant moment before he, too, fell to hit the dust headlong. A cloud of the reddish stuff was raised to mingle with the drift of bluish-gray gunsmoke.

The corpse twitched twice, then lay unmoving. Red spread across the back of the brown vest from a dark exit wound.

The Chinaman fled in silent terror to his cook shack.

Joshua cussed silently. Death had not been his aim, but in a gunfight tricky shooting was seldom more than a fiction, a subsequent fanciful interpretation. When your life or someone else's was in danger, you didn't try cleverly to knock the other fellow's weapon from his grip. You shot at the biggest target — the mass of his torso — and you prayed he'd be disabled before he could kill you.

Gus Kurtz had chosen to make his play with a gun and he was dead.

In swift review, Joshua considered the deputy. He'd been an enigma. Now, he'd never answer the questions he'd raised in Joshua's mind. He was another of the Redstone country's cross-currents Joshua didn't understand.

Why would any deputy be so dedicated in covering his boss's miserable ass? In most constituencies Joshua had known, an ambitious deputy wouldn't lift a finger to help a weak, incompetent or corrupt incumbent in the sheriff's office. He'd work at the opportunity for his own nomination and advancement to the role next election. Paradoxically, Kurtz had also come across as hard-headed and shrewd. He'd been no yes-man.

But it was no moment to mull the mysteries. The cracks of gunfire would have been heard right across the valley,

166

alerting Lant and his returning crew that something had gone awry at the ranch. Even now, they'd be stepping up their horses to a faster gait, hot-hoofing their way to find out what.

He took Liberty by the arm and hurried her past the dead man.

'Don't look. He gave me no choice.'

Reaching the horse corral, Joshua roped a placid-looking gray mare and led it over to where three saddles and other gear had been left draped over a rail outside the harness shed. He threw the best of the rigs across the horse, secured the cinch, put on the bridle and removed the rope.

The mount lived up to expectation. Being of an unexcitable disposition — no snorter or roarer this one — she didn't object to a strange rider any more than she had to a saddle. She pitched only a little and Joshua corrected her frog walking in moments.

'Climb up behind,' he told Liberty, and they rode double downslope to the patch of brush where he'd hitched the sorrel Crazy Bob McGill had brought him from town to Vickers' lakeside cabin.

From that point, Joshua assigned the Flying L gray to Tolliver's rescued wife. His plan was to take her to the protection of whatever friends she must have in Redstone Gulch.

But Liberty wasn't having a bar of that. She had ideas of her own about places of safety.

'The town is full of pigs — human pigs — who curry favor with the Lants and the Flying L. That has been the way of it for years. Everybody is in the Lant pocket, including Sheriff Vickers naturally. No one will dare give me shelter once they know I've crossed them.'

'What about your father?'

'I would only bring trouble to him. Maybe he wouldn't want to know me . . . '

'So what suggestions do you have?'

'Tolliver had a few friends in the badlands. Up in the hills, there's a settlement of sorts called Tall Trees. Maybe I could get a live-in job. It has some stores and a saloon.'

Joshua was uneasy about the proposal, but the time wasn't opportune for argument, nor to point out its possible dangers for an unpartnered woman. After what she'd already been put through, this Tall Trees couldn't hold much worse. Anywhere she went, she was too fine-looking a woman to be left alone, in any sense of the words.

'That means we must take the road out of here west, doesn't it?'

Liberty nodded, and Joshua was perturbed by that, too. It took them in the direction from which Lant and his crew would be returning after they left the cottonwood grove.

Sure enough, it was this fear that was confirmed in short order. The grassland they had to travel over offered insufficient cover to conceal their flight.

One of the Flying L riders must have spotted and drawn attention to them, because the bunch came to a ragged stop. Horses were reined up and turned. Barnaby Lant for one would have recognized who they were — the wife of the man he'd just seen hanged and the man he'd fired for interfering in his affairs in ways he hadn't bargained for.

Somebody yelled, a whole clamor of voices joined in, then the riders reformed and set after them in pursuit.

'We'll have to outrun them,' Joshua snapped. 'Ride like the wind!'

They pointed their mounts for the higher, wilder country, lashing at them with rein ends and kicking at their sides with their heels.

But the Lant crowd raced after them and they gained little if any ground. The chances of capture were high. Out in the open they could be caught and dragged down — roped maybe if any of Lant's hands keenest on their taking possessed the skills.

Joshua shouted, 'We'll never make it to this Tall Trees! They're on our backs and there's no shaking them off. Is

170

there nowhere else? Is your Rocking T any closer?'

Liberty nodded, gasping. 'Yes. Much.'

A clump of piñons loomed ahead, its thickness forming a mass of black shadow.

'There,' Joshua said, jerking his head toward the stand. 'We'll dodge into that timber, weave through, circle out and head for your place. We'll have to make a stand of sorts in the house.'

But what then? he asked himself.

'Maybe some of those fool hellions will calm down and see reason,' he added.

It was hard to put much conviction into the voiced hope. To his own ears, it sounded mighty slim.

★　★　★

Tall Trees was an ugly scar on a bleak landscape further degraded by a failed operation to secure timber for the quick supply of ties to the spreading railroads. Jim Stebbings' arrival in its precincts was noted and word quickly passed, as he had guessed it might be.

A sorry-looking bunch of watchers making a poor pretense of being customers gathered in the big, ramshackle shed that had been converted into the settlement's saloon. These were the men, or their sons, who'd been dispossessed by Old Adam Lant and forced to eke out a living on land harsher than that they considered should still be shared with them. Resentment had festered into hatred. They stared at him.

In the shadowy, dirt-floored room, Jim felt a faint chill touch his spine.

'Looking for something?' he was asked curtly.

He put a coin on the rough deal counter and pushed his hat off his face with a thumb.

'Beer,' he said. 'And words.'

'What makes you think we'd be of a mind to talk with the high 'n' mighty Flying L?'

The inquisitor was a big man with

iron-gray hair, a pocked face and ice-blue eyes. Jim knew him by sight and the name of Donnelly. He had a reputation which said what he lacked in brains, he made up for with his hard, large and knobbly fists. His body and ragged range clothes were dirty. He stank.

Jim cleared his throat. 'I didn't come here ridin' for the brand. I came here as plain Jim Stebbings.'

Donnelly was not impressed. Nor was the group crowding around them, for which he appeared to be the spokesman.

'Explain.'

Jim swallowed beer and let the words tumble out.

Donnelly relaxed some and smiled like a gargoyle, but when Jim got to telling how Tom Tolliver had been lynched while Sheriff Vickers was left toying with his wife at the Flying L ranch house, his mood changed back to suspicion and a heavy frown came to his ugly face.

'Vickers did nothing?'

'Well, no. He's in Lant pay, more or less. Most everyone knows that.'

'Was Gus Kurtz around?'

'Why, yeah, I believe he was, too. But they weren't neither to be seen at the stringing-up of the prisoner.'

The Tall Trees riff-raff exchanged glances that seemed freighted with meaning. Some growled.

Jim interpreted their reaction as sympathy — if these men knew such a sentiment — for Tom and Liberty Tolliver.

Donnelly shook his head heavily, inexpressibly. He turned to his followers.

'Things have been building up and this does it.'

A wind-and-sun-ravaged, string of a man who looked in need of a square meal said, 'We gotta see this for ourselves.'

Jim sensed the mood of the men was restive, bordering on mutinous. Against what?

174

Donnelly said, 'I'm sick of promises. High time we rode on the Flying L anyways. Old Adam's gone and time's a-wasting. Barnaby ain't nothing much, but he's hiring on more gunhawks and killers by the day. Damn' foolish to wait a jot longer.'

Jim was surprised that it had taken so little to stir them into action. It sounded like they were prepared to stage a raid on the strength of the short, grim report they'd let him make.

He didn't know whether he should be glad or dismayed.

Like the rabble they were, the Tall Trees men took no pains or time to organize themselves. In a matter of minutes, they were mounted and supposedly ready to ride on the Flying L.

It struck home to Jim all at once that pinning faith on their foolhardy intervention to rout Lant's hardcases and save Liberty Tolliver was a poor and desperate thing. Though it was futile now, he beat his brains, asking himself what better could he have done.

* ★ *

The Tolliver ranch, when they reached it, was no better or worse a property than Joshua had expected to find. Considerable run down, was his verdict. Albeit squalid and dingy, the wind-weathered log shack showed signs of a woman's pathetic yet ultimately vain attempts to give it the semblance of a home — a vegetable garden to one side, a few yellow and purple wildflowers transplanted to either side of the front door.

But structurally everything about the home was in a state of neglect. The rear wall was out of the perpendicular; flattened tin cans substituting for broken or missing roof shakes had rusted deep, flakey brown to an extent the roof probably leaked again anyway.

It was no time for Joshua to reflect on what any of this told him about the life Liberty had lived here with Tom Tolliver. They'd left clear tracks in and out of the piñons and though the detour had gained them some moments, even dummies would be able to pick up their trail.

They hitched their sweat-streaked horses back of the pole-and-brush shed and plunged into the dim interior of the house. Joshua shut and barred the door and looked around. He found what he wanted in an old Spencer rifle on wall pegs. He took it down, but noted with disapproval its ill-kept appearance.

'Does this thing work?' he asked.

Liberty nodded. 'I think so. There's a box of cartridges someplace . . . '

She rummaged on a shelf of a crudely made dresser with shaking fingers and produced it.

The Spencer was a lever-action repeater with a tube magazine in the buttstock that would hold seven .50 or .52 caliber rimfire cartridges. Many had been sold after the Civil War as government surplus.

Joshua would have preferred to have seen a later-model Winchester capable of firing sixteen shots, fast, without heating its barrel or failing to eject the shell of a cartridge — a fault no earlier repeater had eliminated in rapid use. This piece was of a piece with the man who'd owned it, Joshua reflected, but it could be used to a certain deterrent effect and would have to serve.

With a thunder of hoofs, the Lant bunch wasn't long in arriving. It hove into view with a plan of attack that appeared to amount simply to storming the small cabin.

A cry came on the breeze to the resolute watchers.

'That's Tolliver's dump right ahead, Flyin' L!'

The angry gunnies struck straight and boldly toward the house, eager to come to grips with their tricky quarry.

Before they came within a hundred yards, Joshua sent two heavy slugs on unerring courses. The first downed a horse. The animal collapsed, somersaulting over its forelegs and pitching a Lant gunslinger out of the saddle.

The second shot was more finely

aimed. A Flying L rider was in the act of pulling his long gun from a saddle boot. The shot smashed the stock into splinters.

Consternation raged. The air was made blue with profanities. The attackers pulled back and flung off their broncs, hunting cover and spots and angles of approach that couldn't be commanded from the cabin's small windows.

Joshua felt a brief surge of elation, but he knew at heart the best hope was for a siege. In itself, that was a daunting prospect.

He felt edgy. Could one man and a woman in distress prolong a siege sufficiently for the attackers' hot heads to be cooled? Would wiser counsel eventually prevail?

12

A Choice of Deaths

The Flying L's outlaw recruits were restless as circling wolves. They didn't cotton to any stand-off.

'Hey, Dillard!'

'Well?' Joshua rasped.

'Come on out, Dillard! We want the woman,' Tex Pynchon yelled. 'Give yourselves up and you'll be spared.'

Deep anger seethed within Joshua. His answer was a defiant oath.

'Never, by God!'

A woman had a right to live and move through the world without trash making it a humiliating and degrading experience. Law-abiding or lawless, Western men of character accepted this as part of their code. In some places, it was a matter of pride to show gentlemanly courtesy even to a hussy.

Barnaby Lant gave him back a flat, contemptuous retort.

'The hell you say! I didn't bring you here to meddle in what's private business. You been given the rush, remember? My men can get their hands on you any time they want. The Tolliver female's a rustler's woman.'

'She's her own woman now. Not yours!'

'No, she ain't mine, Mr Dillard, but I answer for myself, not for my boys.'

Provoked by the hint of devious hand-washing in Lant's thick, guttural voice, Joshua sighted the rifle and sent a shot flying close over his shrugging left shoulder. He hoped Lant felt the ominous, whining fan of the slug.

He savvied from his reconnoitering visit to the Flying L cow camp how Barnaby Lant might feel obligated to stand by while his men indulged their natural inclination for devilry. If he didn't, the fighting crew would quit. He'd be left to quell with a handful of regular 'punchers the vengeful strikes of the ranchers his father had wronged.

Lant therefore needed warning.

'You're a perfect target as well as a man of no integrity, Lant,' Joshua called. 'The next slug lifts your hat. The one after that parts your hair — maybe!'

Lant and his hired trash backed off, no one giving, no one waiting for orders. It made not a lick of sense to throw away their lives unnecessarily. Nor were they going to retreat.

They retired in good order and Joshua thought he heard Pynchon's loud mouth suggesting something like 'circle round back'.

Lant tried further parley.

'Dillard, get this straight,' he bellowed. 'You come out with your hands up, unarmed, and we'll do a trade. You get your freedom and I meet all your expenses to get out of the territory.'

'No deal, Lant. It's not my habit to trade with coyotes and snakes.'

'Then you're headin' fer a suicide's grave!' Pynchon declared. 'Stay put with the Tolliver woman and you both get burned out.'

Fire!

The ultimatum, and the confidence with which it was put up, made Joshua's skin crawl.

'Won't work, Pynchon!' he replied with more assertion than the circumstances justified. 'You don't have the makings for torching the place.'

The flimsy argument was met with scornful jeers.

'You'd be plumb surprised, smartass! Tolliver kept a store of coal oil in his brokendown shed an' we found it already!'

Lant said, 'You hear that, Dillard?'

Joshua figured Lant was a bigger fool than he'd already shown himself if he thought he was still running the show. The situation was rapidly getting out of hand.

'Yeah, and this is my answer!'

The shot seemed wasted since he had no visible target, but maybe it would keep Lant's undisciplined crew at bay a few minutes longer.

The echoes of the Spencer's ringing crack died and Liberty said, 'It's gone far enough, Mr Dillard. I don't quite understand why you've bought into my problems though I'm grateful you tried to get me away from Vickers. I think we should now surrender.'

Joshua's immediate instinct was not to have a bar of it.

'No, ma'am! At best, you'd be insulted and mocked. At worst, you'd be the victim of debauchery that'd make Vickers' look like a school boy's. Better perhaps to perish in the flames here than endure the hell they plan. Get down on the floor!'

His imperative wasn't a moment too soon. A volley of shots crashed through a closed but unshuttered window, turning the small pane into flying shards.

Bitterly, he accepted the riled rough-necks were equal to making good their promise to try burning the place around their ears. If they couldn't have their way, then they'd as soon as have their lives. They were men who'd killed before and would again without compunction.

The shots were followed by the thud of booted footfalls approaching at a run. A swirl of flame came through the broken window, igniting a sun-bleached lace curtain as it passed, and fell into the cabin like a small meteor with a tail of oily smoke.

Against the threat of further gunfire, Joshua and Liberty had kept their heads down and a daring hardcase had taken his cue to rush up to the window and throw in a bunch of kindling, soaked in coal oil and blazing.

Joshua rose, put the Spencer to his shoulder and fired a hasty, wasted shot at the man's departing back. Then he had to turn his attention to the firebrand.

Liberty, white-faced but courageously, had leaped up and dashed forward on impulse with a worn throw-rug. She flung it over the burning stuff.

Joshua rushed to stamp on it. For a few seconds it seemed they might succeed in putting out the flames. But the room, being small, quickly filled with choking black smoke.

'Cover your face and get down on the floor again!' Joshua said. The air, he knew, would stay breathable longer there.

Joshua pulled up a bandanna over his own mouth and nostrils and kept stomping.

But horrifyingly, the oily flames caught hold of an edge of the rug and that, too, rapidly became fuel for the fire. Without adequate water at hand, they'd plainly not be able to control it. A blanket or hanging that formed some sort of room divider was next to catch and be consumed.

A long, upended chest — fitted with pine shelves and serving as a makeshift dresser — was engulfed by the licking flames of the twisting, collapsing blanket. Together with its contents, the dresser crashed across an oilcloth-covered table in a shower of sparks.

186

Gallingly, Joshua saw they were beaten. Despite what he'd said about death being preferable to facing the abuse of Lant's bully-boys, he was obliged for the woman's sake to reconsider. Thus far, he'd failed her.

Where she had life, maybe she would have hope. He was forced to make a decision that minutes before would have seemed to go against all sense.

'Our lives aren't worth a prayer if we stay in here,' he said. 'I'm sorry. We'll have to make the best of it, ma'am — take our chances with Lant's mob after all.'

Liberty, coughing, eyes streaming from the irritation of the acrid smoke, couldn't answer other than with a nod.

Joshua figured his own lot was liable to be a volley of deadly gunfire the instant he showed himself. But the real moment of choice had come. If they stayed, Liberty and himself would be roasted alive.

He reloaded the Spencer. He meant to go out and down fighting.

Donnelly and his rabble from Tall Trees had ridden in an approximation of double-file, intent and fast. Jim Stebbings' wearier mount had been hard pressed to keep up with them. The sound of distant gunfire was the first reason they were given for pause.

Jim stiffened in the saddle and a feeling of uneasiness ran through him.

'What was that?' he asked, as the party speculated on the repeated outbreaks of shooting.

A wag said, 'Sure don't signify some sucker out shooting rabbits fer supper!'

Donnelly said, 'Less'n I miss my guess, the vicinity's Tolliver's spread. If Tolliver's hanged like Stebbings says, what the hell's going on? We should go take a look-see.'

He wheeled his claybank with a violent twist of the reins and a fierce gouge of his rowels. The cavalcade gigged its blowing horses back into movement and followed in the fresh direction, veering back toward rougher, rockier country.

Jim trailed along with them, puzzled as they were.

They galloped up a dry watercourse through low hills and came into sight and smell of smoke.

'Look!' Donnelly said. 'Something's doing.'

They thundered on with new vigor and broke into the open on a brush- and boulder-strewn slope above the Tolliver ranch.

'Goddamn! A regular passel of 'em!' someone cried.

The cabin, with smoke pouring from it, was ringed by Flying L riders, the hated Barnaby Lant himself among them.

'Kill them!' Donnelly roared. 'Let them have it, fellers. Death to Lant and his coyote guns!'

Hell broke loose as his rag-tag gang stormed down the slope. The move was foolhardy. Lant's crew, with guns drawn, were seasoned fighters already alert. They swung their weapons to meet the new and unexpected threat.

The result was that though the first skirmish ended slimly to the newcomers' advantage, it was down only to the element of surprise.

Jim Stebbings could have told the men from Tall Trees they'd underestimated their foes. Their brash ill-judgment cost them dearly.

The shooter on horseback is not well-placed for accurate marksmanship. A barrage of hot lead poured in both directions across the open ground, slamming into the flesh of men and animals. Only two of the Lant crew were hit, neither fatally. Meanwhile, the small ranchers' horses reared in panic, stumbled, fell. Ranks were broken.

Confusion resulted as men raced for cover, dropping behind whatever cover they could find. They found themselves mingled amidst their intended targets — the enemy laying siege to the Tolliver cabin — who cut loose on them with Colts and rifles.

And when it came to gunfighting, the Flying L's imported hardcases had the edge in experience and skill.

Jim, who wisely held back, saw Tex Pynchon, a cold grin on his thick lips, confront a hatless and hapless Donnelly. His gun tilted. The shot stopped Donnelly in his tracks.

He dropped to his knees, moaning and clutching hands to a leaking hole in his belly as though he could stop the blood that spurted through his fingers.

'Gawd-a-mighty — gut shot!' he gasped. 'Bastard gut shot me.'

He made a supreme effort, suffering agony, and lurched on to his feet, whereupon Pynchon callously expended another, finishing bullet. It went through his screwed-up face and tore out through the top of his bare head.

Pynchon looked down on the disfigured corpse, his mouth twisting in a sneer of derision.

'That's another won't be battlin' no more.'

In a matter of moments, the aim of

most of the foothills riff-raff was converted to self-preservation.

Abruptly, a new element was added to the wild scene unfolding before Jim's horrified eyes.

The door of the Tolliver house was flung open. Out billowed clouds of smoke; out rushed Joshua Dillard, face hard as granite. He was in a semi-crouch with a Spencer rifle held low in both hands, its butt against his thigh, firing.

On his heels was Liberty Tolliver. A cloth was held to her face, and she was coughing and staggering.

13

Range War!

The area out front of the Tolliver cabin was mad with alarm. Men were running every which way. Fallen horses squealed. On all sides, guns were firing.

How this had come about, Joshua didn't know. From his prior knowledge, he was able to size up a showdown of sorts was at hand between the Flying L outfit and the hardscrabble-rancher aspirants for the Lant family's ill-gotten range.

The daytime raid had been poorly conceived and was less than skillful in execution. It wasn't apt to bring the strugglers from the hills any material gain. But it gave Joshua and Liberty a brief spell to improve on their chances in the dash to escape death by fire, and to regain freedom.

'Follow me!' Joshua said.

The main action between the Flying L and the arrivals had become concentrated around the corral and a patch of scrub to the right. Joshua darted left, toward where he spied a jumble of rocks.

Crouching low, he led Liberty by the hand. They zig-zagged for the chosen spot, running as swiftly as they could bent over.

In the uproar of the clash between the two opposing forces, the escape went unchallenged if not unnoticed. Dust swirled and boiled; the reek of cordite and burning lumber hung on the air. Ideally, Joshua and Liberty should have run directly under the cover of confusion to the horses they'd hitched back of the pole-and-brush shed. But it was uncertain they'd still be there and their first priority was to put distance between themselves and their hunters and the cabin, now well afire.

They reached their objective, breathing heavily, and holed up. Joshua surveyed the scene.

It was a lonesome, rather arid spot where Tolliver had put down roots for his miserable layout. Distantly, mountain peaks reared, ragged and bleakly majestic. The craggy foothills stretching to them were timbered in patches, mostly by pines on southern slopes, but the open land between looked mostly barren of the rich pasture growth that typified Lant's holdings.

Joshua's swift study on the country confirmed in his mind the earlier, ominous impression that such broken terrain wouldn't be a hospitable place for fugitives attempting speedy flight from resolute pursuers.

Lant's desperadoes had assumed the upper hand in the gunfight. Joshua judged it wouldn't take long to shoot itself out. The newcomers evidently had begun with marginal superiority of numbers, but they'd walked into a trap of their own making — Lant's professional killers were never going to be easily dislodged and trounced — and losing their leader had sapped their morale.

Most were unhorsed and no retreat was open to them. The outcome was just a matter of time.

One by one the men from the hills lost heart and stomach for a fight which could end only one way. Some tried to slip away at a first favorable opportunity or during lulls in the exchanges of fire. It served them ill. Joshua saw two who tried to light a shuck buy themselves a bullet in the back.

Rage rose and stormed in him. He had to get Liberty away from here fast, before the rout of the hill-country army by the gunslicks was complete. They needed a horse, preferably two. Several animals roaming about with empty saddles looked likely prospects.

'Stay here and keep your head down,' he told Liberty. 'I aim for us to ride out of here.' He handed her the rifle.

Liberty's face paled and her lips moved stiffly.

'Are you sure it's for the best? They'll

gun you down soon as they notice you.'

'True, but we won't get far on our own legs. They'd track us down in no time.'

The brief summation of their continuing predicament was the end of argument, for he darted out from the rocks to new cover — a horse shot dead in the early stages of the battle. A coiled rope was still attached to the saddle. Joshua unhitched it and pulled it out from under the carcass.

The loose horses, spooked by the commotion of gunplay, had moved away from the cabin's front yard. One or two, going by the numbers, must have kept right on going. Joshua shook out a loop and made a cast for a dun gelding that was closest to the rocks and showed the least signs of agitation.

His bid to lasso the horse might have succeeded had he not been spied by Lant's foreman, grumpy Carl Pederson. Seeking to re-establish some small part of his eroding authority, Pederson pointed.

'Look, fellers — Dillard! The inter-ferin' sonofabitch is fixin' to get away!'

His cry turned hasty gunfire in Joshua's direction. The shots were wild, missing him. But one creased the dun's hide and it took off at the critical moment. The noose of Joshua's lariat brushed harmlessly across its back and off its hindquarters.

Joshua dropped the rope and his hand streaked for the holster at his side. He palmed the Peacemaker, swinging it up and swinging himself to face the multiple gunmen in a single movement.

Death had never seemed closer, more inevitable.

What saved him was totally unex-pected. Liberty Tolliver intervened. A wild and startling sight, she rushed from the rock pile, the cumbersome Spencer to her shoulder.

'Stop!' she yelled. 'I can use this thing, and Mr Pederson will die first!'

She took up a stance in front of Joshua, blocking him from the Lant guns. Though her rifle had the distinct advantage of light recoil, and she had the sights aligned right on Pederson, it was very heavy, over ten pounds loaded. Putting herself directly in the line of fire was the craziest of plays.

'This thing is over,' she said, and Joshua was amazed by the firmness in her tone. 'I've taken enough. I'll be dead before you can touch me, but so will some of yours.'

For a brief moment, astonishment froze Lant's fighters, too. Whoever shot at Joshua was likely to plug Liberty instead, and wasn't the woman their promised bounty? Killing her would make a man a mite unpopular with his sidekicks.

The madness saved Joshua but not the day.

Two hardcases moved in on her, cautiously, either side. She went to use the Spencer as she'd threatened, but the weighty weapon produced a sound that reached Joshua's ears as only a feeble click.

What had happened, he didn't know.

Possibly a double feed had jammed the gun, a failure not uncommon when the lever wasn't operated smoothly. Or given the gun's age and condition, a weak magazine spring might be to blame.

'Grab the rifle!' Pederson bawled.

The pair moving in on Liberty did.

'That's too much gun for too much woman,' one said with a humorless laugh. 'Mebbe I oughta take it offa yuh, honey, jest fer safety!'

Liberty gave a pained cry. The Spencer was wrenched from her hold. The two were joined by others as soon as the confiscation was accomplished, laying their hands on softer prizes, serving notice of the insufferable attentions they had in store for her.

Though her eyes were bright with fear and unvoiced pleading was on her writhing lips, Joshua was helpless to intercede. His thinking was dominated by the realization that within minutes he could be dead. He tensed, waiting for the shot or shots that would end it all.

But again attention was switched from him.

Barnaby Lant emitted a growl of wrath like a maddened bear.

'It's Stebbings, men! Look — it's him to blame! The turncoat brought the rabble down on us. Stop him!'

The remnants of the Tall Trees force, including Jim Stebbings, were taking advantage of the diversion created by Liberty Tolliver's capture. With all the Lant bunch's eyes riveted on the distressed woman's struggles, they were mounting up and riding out.

Maybe because Carl Pederson was best familiar with responding to the snarls of his morose boss, or because he had less of an appetite for tormenting a woman, his reactions were the fastest.

Pederson stooped and swept up the uncoiled lariat with which Joshua had tried to dab a loop on the loose dun. He cast the rope after Jim Stebbings.

Unlike most of his companions, Pederson was a long-practised cowman. The spinning noose curved across the intervening space as Jim kneed his horse into a trot. It seemed to hover momentarily, then it fell. Though a tricky throw, it settled right over its target.

It passed over the young 'puncher's shoulders to tighten around him, pinning his arms. Jim tried to pull up, but the horse kept going following the other escaping horses.

Pederson dug the heels of his riding boots into the ground; the rope went taut. Jim was dragged out of the saddle while his panicked horse went on.

He hit the dust heavily.

Cheers and jeers erupted from the Lant pack. Pederson was too angry at his hand's defection from the Flying L brand to join in any merriment. He wound in the lariat, hauling Jim bodily over the ground.

'Damn you, Jim Stebbings!' he said. 'What the hell's the game? You'll get your walking papers for this . . . That's if'n the boys let you live!'

14

Knowing Too Much

'They know about the lynching of Tom Tolliver. Maybe plenty else besides . . . Seems like we'll have to kill the three of them,' Sheriff Vickers said, nigh on spitting the words through his punch-swollen lips. 'Ain't that a shame?'

Vickers repeatedly held a hand to the back of his neck and twisted his head from side to side as though to check the movement was still possible. He regarded Joshua Dillard, the man who'd dealt him his injuries, with undisguised hatred. His eyes brimmed hotly with it.

The hardcase core of the Flying L crew had crowded with their prisoners, Joshua Dillard, Liberty Tolliver and Jim Stebbings, into the big parlor of the Lant ranch house.

Joshua regarded it as a minor miracle that he'd been spared summary execution, but it seemed his degenerate captors had motives to explain that.

Barnaby Lant, never by nature his bold father's son, feared word might spread of his outfit's ruthless activities after the battle with the smaller ranchers and the escape of a few survivors of the rag-tag army from Tall Trees. He didn't want the inconvenience of providing explanations to outside authorities. Far better the whole affair should be glossed over; all evidence of extra-judicial execution eliminated.

Thus he had made known, in flat, emotionless tones, his desires and the method by which they should be accommodated.

'Before Dillard and Stebbings die, they should dig graves for themselves, Tolliver and his woman. And it don't need saying, once they're filled, the graves stay unmarked.'

Dan Vickers endorsed the proposals,

grinning widely. 'Good! Just what I wanted to hear.' He made no mention of his badge-packing partner, Gus Kurtz.

Joshua wondered if the sheriff knew Kurtz had been shot dead after he, Vickers, had been chopped down senseless. Joshua also remained puzzled about the deputy's unswerving loyalty to a chief not fit to be in office when good sense argued he should have been preparing to run for election in his stead.

Additionally, although it was no longer his concern, Joshua could figure no logical explanation for the organized plundering of the Flying L herds. He had now witnessed the strength — and the weakness — of the hill folk for himself. They were men with grudges against Lant, eking out a livelihood on the poorest of land. Lant's father, hard old Adam Lant, had built his Flying L spread by climbing roughshod over them, and they'd feared him. It was possible they had a fear of Barnaby

Lant, too, though instinct must have told them he was a weaker man — vulnerable were it not for his new-found propensity for hiring gunslingers and cold-blooded mercenaries.

But wholesale cattle theft as part of their retaliation?

Joshua thought not and the rustling remained the larger mystery. Down-trodden, impoverished trash such as he'd seen in the fight at the Tolliver ranch would have been incapable of masterminding the operation. And where could they have marketed branded beeves without bills of sale?

Tex Pynchon and his sidekicks baulked only at the finer details of timing for Lant's plan of murder. They weren't satisfied with the drudgery of the cowboying life, even at gun-hands' wages. Having tasted action of a kind more to their liking, they lusted for a sampling of the trimmings and spoils that armies throughout the ages had always taken from the defeated.

'Hold on!' Pynchon said. 'Not so

fast, gents. The boys don't tie to the plan.'

'What the hell's wrong with what Mr Barnaby says?' Vickers asked.

'It ain't that we don't latch on to cuttin' their water off, but we figure to git some fun outa life first, an' we had ourselves a square deal concernin' the woman. Someone's liable to git a shuck in their snoot if'n the word ain't kept. Lant can live like a monk hisself, but he can't expect that of the boys.'

Rage boiled in Joshua. Protest would be fruitless, of course, and his hands were tied — very securely with strips of rawhide. God knew what these scum would subject Liberty to, but he'd give ten to one she'd prefer a quick death.

Vickers said, with a trace of impatient scorn, 'Maybe she won't be much reward, fellers . . . looks kinda played out already.'

'Yeah, you already had your turns, I reckon,' Pynchon said, all sneering sarcasm. 'You ain't stoppin' no one havin' theirs. You button your lip, *lawman*.'

Vickers laughed — a short, brittle laugh — resigned to the delay. He shrugged.

'Well, she jumped the broomstick way back with Tolliver. She's been put on her back, or her hands and knees, times enough to know how to unlimber, I guess. Help yourselves.'

'Wise,' Pynchon approved.

Liberty was white-lipped; shaken. And silent, till she was made aware of the gang's exact intentions.

Pynchon said, 'Cut her loose, Luke. She can start the show by takin' her clothes off.'

'What!' she cried.

'Missus, we know you ain't no babe in a state o' blind ignorance. Git 'em off. Start with the shoes 'n' stockings.'

'I will not!'

Luke severed the ties binding her wrists. Pynchon stuck out his hand.

'Gimme your knife, Luke. Seem to

remember the lady didn't wanna see this Dillard feller's blood spilled quick with bullets. Mebbe if we was to slice his goddamn' throat, she'd be more obligin'.'

Pynchon went behind Joshua, took a twisting grip on a handful of hair and pressed the knife to his Adam's apple.

Joshua grunted.

'Don't watch, Mrs Tolliver. Ignore him!'

'Keep your trap shut, brave man!' Pynchon said, and shifted the knife to score the skin with its point. Beads of blood erupted along the scratch and Joshua experienced the smarting sensation of the broken skin.

Liberty gasped. 'No!'

'No, little lady? Well, you know what to do.'

'You monsters!' she blurted, but she kicked off her shoes and reached under her skirt.

Low chuckles of lewd appreciation greeted her surrender to their demands.

Joshua was possessed by well-nigh

ungovernable fury. He was helpless to intervene. He breathed hard through his nose, his nostrils flaring.

'Refuse the bastards!' he croaked.

'I said shuddup!' Pynchon reminded him harshly.

'I can't,' Liberty sobbed. 'There's been too much death already. Do you want me to watch more?'

Luke said, 'The blouse — take off the blouse!'

She hesitated; the men crowding round her murmured threateningly.

'Go on!' Pynchon snarled. 'Do as he tells you!'

Liberty began undoing buttons with trembling fingers.

What else could she do but obey them? It was madness to argue.

Joshua looked for Barnaby Lant. By swiveling his eyes, he found him at a sideboard sloshing liquor from a heavy cut-glass decanter into a fist-sized glass. The cattleman tossed the whiskey down in a single gulp, then began pouring another.

Joshua saw scant hope for any intervention.

It was payoff time. Lant had no illusions about the loyalty of his new hands. They followed his orders because he paid them well, treated them well. They'd been virtually promised the bonus of fun with Liberty Tolliver. He couldn't back down on it. They were tired of playing at being cowhands.

Their customary relaxation would be drinking, gambling and perhaps a woman in a saloon. Work on a cattle-ranch with lodging in a bunkhouse had deprived them too long.

'Now unhitch your skirt,' Luke was saying.

'But I'm not what you th — ' Liberty began.

'Do you really want me to slash your pal's throat?' Pynchon cut in.

'This is crazy,' Joshua mumbled, virtually to himself. He could feel the tension and the arousal of the hungry men; smell their feverish sweat.

What made them believe they were entitled to humiliate a young woman for their excitement, their pleasure? He wondered how some could be so violent to women and others never were.

'Lant!' he said desperately. 'Are you going to allow your pack to do this?'

Lant cleared his throat. His speech was slurred.

'The woman is a robust ranch woman, mister. She can take it. I seen her with Vickers. She got a fine body — strong legs and thighs.'

Joshua gritted his teeth in exasperation.

The attitude was prevalent. Robust health and the color from outdoor living were presumed to indicate a low, willing woman; lack of exercise, indoor confinement and a pale complexion were seen as ladylike.

Joshua heard the soft rustle of Liberty's skirt as it fell. She was down to a chemise and drawers. The hands gloated and hooted in ribald excitement.

'Yeah, she's tendin' buxom,' someone responded to Lant's comment. 'Full nude she'll be purtier'n an oil paintin' in a fancy saloon!'

Joshua could guess how it would unfold from here on. The stripping was just the overture. Liberty Tolliver would be required to meet other demands from her tormentors once they grew tired of mere gawking.

Glinting-eyed, the more impatient were making testing forays, to steal kisses, feel, pinch and squeeze as she squirmed in her underwear.

'Let the slut git on with it!' Pynchon said. 'When she's nekkid, we'll draw cards to see who gits first poke.'

But the dream of the outlaw trash and the nightmare of their victim was never to reach a climax. For unnoticed amid the mounting ribaldry a buckboard had rattled to a slithering halt in the yard outside.

Dan Vickers, less interested in Liberty's show, said, 'Sounds like we've got company.'

And two disheveled, hot and dusty figures burst in on the proceedings.

* * *

The arrivals were Crazy Bob McGill and Vickers' wife, Sophie.

They came pushing through the door together, as though fighting to be first on the scene.

Crazy Bob had never looked less adequate to cope with the vicissitudes of a world no longer quite within his aging comprehension. Other persons' behavior at a relationship level was his or her business, and he didn't really want to be shocked by knowing about anyone's illicit activity, but what did a father do when it involved his own daughter?

Stumbling on his bad leg, he was shoved aside by his incensed and determined escort.

'Look out, gents!' he blurted. 'Missus Vickers made me bring her, and she's off her rocker!'

Joshua experienced a cold thrill of shock. He strained without results at his bound wrists, and sweat started out in beads on his forehead.

Sophie was armed again with her derringer. How, Joshua didn't know. She flourished it impetuously. Her eyes flashed dangerously.

'I'm going to blow your head off, Daniel Vickers!' she said in excitable, shrill tones.

Joshua, looking into her face, found proof there of something which he'd only partly suspected. The sheriff's wife was mad. She was a ruthless maniac with a gun.

If anyone in the room was insane, it wasn't the maligned Crazy Bob, or Sophie's depressive brother Barnaby Lant, or his rape-minded crew, or her philandering husband, Vickers. It was Sophie, and he was powerless to do a thing about it.

Rage and hate and anguish had robbed her of sense.

'You're a dirty, unfaithful dog, and an

insult to me, your badge and the community,' she went on.

'Now, Sophie,' Vickers began. 'Think what — '

'No, you think! And if you think I'm bluffing, think again. Just look at your brazen young harlot! I see you have her here in a disgusting state of undress and on her proper level — a toy to dangle before ignorant, hired men . . . *Think again!*'

Sophie's gun arm came up. Her knuckle whitened around the derringer's trigger.

Vickers put up his hands as though to ward off the bullet. His voice was shrill with fear. 'God, woman — I swear she never meant a thing to me!'

But while Sophie was running off at the mouth, her brother, a man conversely of few words and most of them sullen, had gathered his wits.

Lant threw his ponderous weight across the space that separated him from his sister. He grabbed at her wrist and the gun, shoving her off balance.

The little pistol's snout snarled death from one of its three-and-a-half inch barrels. But in delivering her diatribe of marital condemnation, Sophie had delayed too long. Because of Lant's interference, the shot went wild.

The cut-glass decanter on the side-board exploded in flying splinters.

It was the second time Lant had wrested the gun from Sophie and this time he kept it tightly in his big fist. But Sophie was far from finished. She recovered her footing and went for him tooth and nail.

'Get her off me!' Lant barked.

It took Pynchon to do it. Everybody else seemed shocked into immobility. He flung Luke's knife and Joshua aside.

The knife embedded itself, quivering, in the stuffing of a couch; Joshua, hands tied and unable to save himself, was hurled in an opposite direction to the floor and came up bone-crunchingly hard against the solid mahogany side-board.

Pynchon went to the ranch boss's

rescue. Even then, Sophie struggled and kicked, spat and cursed.

'You're a fool, Barnaby! Give me my gun and let me kill the sonofabitch!'

'Stop this, Sophie!'

Though held fast by Pynchon, Sophie was beside herself, the fury running hot and violent in her blood.

'Why are you interfering?' she ranted incredulously. 'You're my own brother and had the gall to leave me restrained — tied up! — at the bastard's lakeside love-nest!'

'It was for your own good, Sophie. You were beside yourself, uncontrollable . . . like now.'

Mouths agape, the crew watched the developing family quarrel, not entirely insensitive to its import and impropriety.

'I hate your ways, big brother, and all you stand for!' Sophie retorted. 'It's why I'll be glad when they trample over you! After father died, you shut me out of the running of the Flying L at every turn!'

'You were a woman, Sophie,' Lant said, as though that might explain everything. 'Besides, you always preferred town life to ranch life. You couldn't wait to get away.'

'Tchah! I'm a businesswoman, too. You had no excuse for denying me a say.'

'It's the way Pa willed it.'

'He should've known the responsibility of running an outfit as big as the Flying L was no job for a *weak* person!'

Resentment darkened Lant's face.

Nor had Sophie finished saying her piece. She had more shocks to spring.

'Barnaby, you must be utterly stupid! Worse than most anyone knows!'

'What does that crack mean?'

'I'll tell you, then maybe you won't be so hot on shielding my precious husband . . . '

Intriguing though this exchange was, Joshua was putting equal attention into freeing his hands. Although Sophie's teeth had been drawn, he had a shrewd inkling events were about to come to a boiling-over that would leave no one in the room untouched.

His groping fingers had located a shard of the broken whiskey decanter. He was concentrating on manipulating it so he could use its sharp edges to sever the rawhide around his wrists.

Already he'd cut himself several times and the glass was greasy with his blood. But he bore the stinging hurts stoically, betraying nothing of his efforts.

'You're an idiot, Barnaby,' Sophie prattled on. 'In your position, only a soft-brain would've missed the signs and not figured it out long past. The secret leader of the opportunists rustling the Flying L blind is my dear husband and your loyal lawdog!'

A startled exclamation left Lant's lips, but he appeared struck speechless.

Sophie snorted contemptuously.

'Yes, Dan Vickers is the man masterminding the operations against you, though in his familiar way he left the gritty chore of conveying orders to the foothills trash to someone else — his equally corrupt deputy!'

As Joshua struggled to manipulate the sliver of glass behind his back, part of what had been puzzling him about the set-up in the Redstone sheriff's office abruptly became that much clearer:

Of course — Gus Kurtz had also been Vickers' lieutenant and partner in crime. For Kurtz to challenge Vickers would have risked whatever profits that brought him, and risked his own safety.

Sophie continued, 'Gus Kurtz was my husband's eyes and ears, keeping him informed of the mood in the country and recruiting the riders who did the menial work of driving the stolen herds to the buyers.' She laughed ironically. 'Can you imagine either of them hazing cow brutes? Meantime, as Gus kept watch on that dirty business, dear Daniel would be gone fishing — and we've seen what that meant: dirty doings of another kind!'

She tried to wrench free of Pynchon's

hold, but he was too strong for her.

'And tell your ape to get his hands off me, Barnaby! He stinks worse than skunk!'

Some of Pynchon's sidekicks sniggered. Pynchon, who had a pride of sorts, flushed angrily.

'Button your lip, you high 'n' mighty bitch!'

He brought the back of his hand across Sophie's face. The sound of it was sharp as a rifle shot.

She yelped in outrage. 'Barnaby! Will you let me be struck by your hired help?'

But Lant was no longer listening to her. His features were frozen and only a staring, distant fixity in his gaze evidenced the huger affront he'd suffered.

Joshua could imagine the course of his thoughts. One thing a big rancher expected was loyalty. Barnaby Lant would have grown up seeing it constantly in the cowpunchers who rode for his father's brand. In the cattle territories of the West, it was the code. You stood with your own — with your ranch and your fellow crew and your boss. There was no room for deviation from the over-riding requirement. The man who tried to buck it became an outcast, a pariah.

Dan Vickers was a part of the Lant outfit. Nothing more. He owed his office and his status entirely to the machinations of old Adam Lant. Apart from a strict adherence to protecting the Lant interests in community and political affairs, he'd been expected to contribute little else to the family in return. Moreover, Adam had awarded him his not-unattractive daughter as a kind of bonus. But all this, apparently, had not been enough.

'Poor, credulous Barnaby!' Sophie added, recognizing her brother's distraction for what it was and turning the knife with sarcastic relish. 'A share of the money for Pa's herds came to me anyway!'

Vickers had been staring at the Lant

pair as though hypnotized. Now he gave a sick grin and tried to shrug off his wife's damning revelations.

'Well,' he said wheedlingly into an ominous near-silence, 'the air's surely cleared now. I guess we can make a deal, Barnaby. Sophie's right. You couldn't hold all that range together. It was — is — too big for any one man 'cept Old Adam.'

Sophie scoffed. 'Don't listen to the two-timer, Barnaby! Why, I've seen more of the money from rustled Flying L beef than you ever will!'

But hearing the slighting comparison with his father voiced openly to his face, and in front of his fascinated crew, was the last straw for Lant. The unwelcome truth was too much for him.

For a moment, Lant's heavy lower lip sagged, then his mouth pulled in and the only sound was a deep-throated growl.

The Remington derringer enclosed in his big right mitt swung up and its stubby snout pointed.

15

Finishing Shots

Dan Vickers stared into the raised muzzle of the tiny but deadly gun at the end of Lant's outstretched arm; saw a thick finger tightening on the trigger. The smirk was wiped from his face and Joshua saw the unapologetic schemer and womanizer disintegrate into a coward on the edge of hysteria.

Vickers realized he was a defenseless dude surrounded by villains of a stripe that had never given a damn what happened to him. With no one to protect him, death was only seconds away.

Joshua tugged frantically at the rawhide around his wrists. Though frayed by the cut glass, it still wouldn't give. Damn it! Any moment, lead would fly and who knew how it would end? With the killings of trapped innocents like Liberty, Crazy Bob and Jim Stebbings? Of himself?

Vickers raised his hands imploringly and screamed for mercy.

'No, Barnaby, no! It was a bad call — a terrible mistake. I'll pay you b — '

'Enough, you slimy piece of goose-flesh!' Lant snarled.

His voice charged with hate, infuriated by how he'd been duped by the family's supposed catspaw, Lant fired the derringer at close range.

The treacherous sheriff was flung backwards under the impact of the .41 bullet. He hit a wall, folded down on to his knees, and keeled over on the floor. Blood pumped from a neat hole in his coat just below the badge he'd never deserved to pin on it.

For a brief moment, Vickers' tear-filled eyes fixed abjectly on the face of his killer. He didn't last long. With pain and blood loss, the stare quickly became glassy. And dead.

Simultaneously, Joshua's bonds snapped. He jumped up and delivered a tooth-busting uppercut to the jaw of the nearest hardcase engrossed — as they all were — in the sudden, violent demise of the Sheriff of Redstone. As the man slumped, he wrestled to drag the six-shooter from the holster low on his hip.

Sophie was laughing hysterically. Tex Pynchon, supposing the danger from her to be past with the death of her despised spouse, let her go and returned his attention to Joshua with a bellow.

'Don't try it, Dillard!'

Joshua turned to find himself looking into the muzzle of the Texas gunfighter's Colt. He froze. His only chance of turning the tables and taking command of the situation was gone.

But he reckoned without Sophie.

As Crazy Bob and he himself had earlier assessed, the woman had become seriously unhinged. With Pynchon's back turned to her, she intended to have an excess of bloody revenge for the manhandling and slapping she'd suffered from the gunhawk.

With a manic cry, she pulled Luke's long knife from the couch cushion where Pynchon had tossed it and threw all her weight into plunging it deeply, viciously, into his back.

The hammer of Pynchon's Colt fell and the gun roared, but he was pitching forward and the bullet ripped into the floorboards a foot from Joshua's booted left toe.

He gave one ghastly screech, dropped the gun and tried to reach behind him. But he couldn't remove the source of the burning, breathtaking agony; the knife handle protruded only inches from his back. He flopped to the floor on his ashen face and blood seeped through his clenched lips. It became a trickle, then a torrent as he went lax and his mouth gaped open.

Joshua hefted the KO'd gunhawk's six-shooter in his fist and swung it threateningly.

'Leave it! Keep those hands still, the lot of you!'

But Pynchon had been the real leader

here — not the ramrod Pederson, not Lant. Nobody else wanted a fight. Nobody had a life they figured was worth losing in what had fast taken on the makings of a personal, profitless feud.

Except Barnaby Lant himself. Backing down was something he'd never had to learn how to do.

He hadn't forgotten the Remington pistol he'd used on Vickers was a two-shot. He chucked it in Joshua's face and hauled his trustier Smith & Wesson from leather. But he miscalculated the gunspeed necessary to stop Joshua from aiming and firing his appropriated weapon.

Joshua fended off the flying chunk of pretty, nickel-finished, pearl-gripped and discharged gun metal with his left forearm. At the same time, the gun in his right hand flamed as one with the Smith & Wesson.

The occupants of the room gasped as the place rocked to the guns' ear-splitting twin thunder. A moment of silence followed for deafened ears, then Lant's gun fell with a thump from lifeless fingers. Joshua's slug had traveled true to the cattleman's black heart. His big frame seemed to crumple with painful slowness. He had an unfocused stare of stupid surprise on his broad, flat face.

The bore of his black-barreled Smith & Wesson had centered at the instant of firing high on a plastered facing wall. His bullet had drilled a hole surrounded by a drunken spider's web of cracks.

When Lant's heavy body hit the floorboards, the place rocked anew. A door swung with a creak and windows rattled.

Joshua stood firm as a rock, legs braced slightly apart, holding the long, smoking forty-five steady in his fist, ready to swivel wherever his attention might be needed.

He said, 'Anyone else is welcome to the same, though God help him.'

Lips were licked and heads shook.

No one took up the challenge.

The Lant crew were not especially afraid of a fight, Joshua figured, but they were professionals — gunhawks and outlaws whose paths had long been down devious trails on which they'd honed the intuitive ability to choose time and place for their actions. The man who'd been paying them was dead. Why put life on the line?

'Then I think we can say it's over, gentlemen,' Joshua said.

Then, remembering manners and the two women unfortunately present, plus their sad parts in the affair, he added with a deferential nod, 'And ladies.'

* * *

Some hours later, when the Lant gunnies had ridden out, and the bodies and the blood were removed from the ranch-house, Joshua Dillard and Jim Stebbings built themselves cigarettes and quietly filled in the gaps in the story.

231

Joshua would have liked to have brought the Flying L's toughs to account for their persecution of Liberty Tolliver, but it wasn't a task he could tackle single-handed.

Pragmatically, he observed to Jim, 'Law in the West frequently goes unenforced and justice often comes from the barrel of a gun. There was nothing more we could do.'

Jim flatteringly insisted on regarding Joshua as an 'undercover range detective' rather than a down-and-out adventurer. He took a modicum of pride in being able to piece together for him the background to the rustling operation as he had learned it from the multiply aggrieved small fry of the hill spreads.

'When they thought Dan Vickers was betrayin' 'em, you saw how they came hot-foot and hot-headed, spoilin' for a fight.'

Jim explained how, after the death of despotic old Adam Lant, Dan Vickers had seen a chance of better feathering his nest than in standing by his less effective son. The key was the railroads pushing across Montana and their temporary construction camps.

By day and sometimes into the night, great gangs of men, mules and oxen could be observed on the fills and grades like swarms of ants. Landscapes would shudder as heavy charges of explosives blew off the sides of hills or loosened ridges to push the cuts through.

All the digging and carrying of rock and dirt had to be done by men with picks, shovels and wheelbarrows. It was tiring, hot, dusty work that burned up a lot of energy. Come full dark, the hungry crews packed the company feed tents in the ragged tent towns.

The get-rich-quick caterers and their butchers were no fussier than the crooks who ran the camps' more plainly corrupt gambling and drinking dives, or the euphemistically named 'dance halls' with wooden floors and canvas roofs and painted honkytonk girls. No questions were asked when the over-riding aim was to profit from the demanding appetite of a temper-frayed Irishman who'd spent his day laying track, swinging a hammer or drilling and blasting rock. Ragtown food businesses offered cows at a good price didn't look closely into falsified brands or ask to see bills of sale. It was cash on the barrel-head. They didn't care if their purchases were of dubious legality.

'Well, I guess any evidence was eaten in short order,' Joshua commented.

Jim drew smoke from his cigarette and tied up the last loose ends.

'Vickers and Kurtz weren't cowmen. Like Sophie said, they roped in the labor to run the hands-on side of the operation from among the old enemies Adam Lant had pushed out to back-country poverty. The sheriff's office in Redstone gave Vickers the cover and a headquarters from where he fixed shipment of the cattle across the mountains to his shifting markets.'

Joshua grinned ruefully. 'It all clicks

into place. I should've figured out the answers for myself, but Kurtz's attack on Crazy Bob and Vickers' abuse of his daughter at the Devil's Lake cabin had me sidetrailed from the word go.'

'But I was *told* this stuff,' Jim said stoutly. 'You're the real detective here.'

Joshua raised his eyebrows and sighed. 'I don't know about that.'

He stayed around long enough in Redstone to see things settled down and no range war apt to break out.

He was pleased when Liberty shifted from the lonely, burned-out Rocking T into Crazy Bob's house, making both her peace with her father and needed improvements in his housekeeping.

Joshua also noted Jim Stebbings was a frequent caller at Crazy Bob's.

When word came by wire from a friend in Denver of another likely job for him, Joshua prepared to hit the trail. Any business he'd had here was over and he felt little sorrow in his heart and, as was invariably the case in his footloose life, no money in his pockets either.

Before he left he told Jim dryly, 'I don't need to be a real detective to figure out that one day soon you're going to make Liberty a better husband than she ever had in Tom Tolliver.'

Jim dropped his head and scratched the dirt with a boot toe awkwardly.

'You really think I'm the right feller?'

Joshua said, 'Do yourself, Liberty and the world a favor. Just put the question to her!'

THE END

We do hope that you have enjoyed reading this large print book.

Did you know that all of our titles are available for purchase?

We publish a wide range of high quality large print books including:
Romances, Mysteries, Classics
General Fiction
Non Fiction and Westerns

Special interest titles available in large print are:
The Little Oxford Dictionary
Music Book, Song Book
Hymn Book, Service Book

Also available from us courtesy of Oxford University Press:
Young Readers' Dictionary
(large print edition)
Young Readers' Thesaurus
(large print edition)

For further information or a free brochure, please contact us at:
Ulverscroft Large Print Books Ltd.,
The Green, Bradgate Road, Anstey,
Leicester, LE7 7FU, England.
Tel: (00 44) **0116 236 4325**
Fax: (00 44) **0116 234 0205**

Other titles in the
Linford Western Library:

A MAN NAMED SHONTO

Ryan Bodie

They were already hanging Marshal Holder when Shonto rode into town. It was one hell of a welcome for a loner with a gun but Shonto sensed that things were going to get even worse. He was right. The marshal's body was still swinging from the cottonwood across the street from his own jailhouse when the town became a bloody battleground. At that point, Shonto had just two choices: shoot to kill or join the lawman in hell.

WIND RIDER

Thomas McNulty

The Sioux call him Wind Rider . . . Hank Benteen rides into trouble in a Wyoming valley after saving the lives of a homesteader and his children. A range war is brewing and some of the cowboys are hiding a murderous secret. Then, resolving to safeguard the homesteaders' properties, Benteen becomes involved in a deadly game with two avaricious men, intent on acquiring land by brute force. The Wind Rider will need all his skills as a gunman to survive . . .

THE LEGACY

Logan Winters

There was nothing special about the J-Bar ranch in Colorado . . . except that it had thirty thousand acres of prime land and its previous owner had just been murdered, leaving $50,000 in hidden gold. Then the whole territory joined the hunt for the missing fortune; violence and murder became commonplace. But then three heirs arrived from the East — and that is when true chaos erupted . . .

ROBBERY IN SAVAGE PASS

D. M. Harrison

Soames Ho accepts work from a Pinkerton agent, to take gold from Marysville to a Californian bank. But the driver of the stagecoach carrying the gold is nervous; the shotgun rider a greenhorn. They travel through Savage Pass, only to face three men intent on robbery. But the Pinkerton agent's deliberate plan, to have an ineffectual escort for the stagecoach, underestimates Soames. He believes in justice, and whatever the cost, he's determined to find the gold and the outlaws.

THE DEVIL's GOLD

M. Duggan

Dennis Rumble wasn't a good man — but he wasn't entirely bad — unlike the notorious band of outlaws calling themselves the Coyotes, into whose territory he was obliged to travel. He was on a mission to rescue a beautiful woman snatched from the stage by the outlaws. But things are not always as they seem. Twists and turns lay ahead of him and many men were destined to lose their lives over what Rumble called 'The Devil's Gold'.